SECRETS AND PROMISES

Jane Anthony

Secrets and Promises
Copyright © Jane Anthony 2016
All rights reserved

Cover Design by:
Marisa Shor, Cover Me, Darling

Editing by:
Nichole Strauss, Perfectly Publishable

Proofreading by:
Jenny Sims, Editing 4 Indies

Formatting by:
Christine Borgford, Perfectly Publishable

For JT, AT & LT

CHAPTER ONE

Jillian

"SURE. JUST A minute, lemme check the schedule." I swiveled my chair around to face the ancient computer on the desk and tapped a few keys waiting for the program to load. *God, this thing takes forever.* When the appointment calendar finally popped up, I turned back to the phone. "Do you wanna bring it in tomorrow morning?" I asked the caller. "Ford Mustang, 1965, right? Okay, great, you're all set. Yep, we open at nine. Thank you!"

I hung up and quickly plotted in the appointment. *Oil change, 1965 Ford Mustang, 9 am.*

The guy on the phone sounded unusually young. In my experience, guys who owned classic cars were just as old as the cars themselves. No one even remotely attractive ever walked in here. It was all old gear heads or moms with mini vans who needed tune-ups.

I rubbed my eyes and stretched before standing to let AJ know I was getting ready to head out for lunch. As if on cue, he walked out of the shop, and into the small, attached office.

"Jillian, Mr. Willard's brake job is done. Give him a call and let him know he can come pick it up this afternoon." I nodded to my big brother and sat back down to call Mr. Willard.

AJ had grease all over his coveralls and embedded in his fingernails. He'd been burning the candle at both ends trying to keep the family business running while saving money to send me to college. I was all set to start last year when our dad had a sudden heart attack and passed away in his sleep.

I'd been working in the office forever, and even though he protested, I insisted I was skipping school, for now, to stay and help. College would always be there, but Morello and Son's Restoration didn't have that luxury.

Anthony Morello, Sr. built this business from dirt and sweat when he was just about as old as my brother was. My mom, Gabby, and he worked the way AJ and I did—her in the office and him in the garage. It was a family business, and my dad prided himself on that.

We lived in the small colonial behind the property and every memory from my childhood included this dirty shop. It ran the gamut of basic car repairs—gaskets to transmission rebuilds—but my dad's true passion was restoring the vintage vehicles. My dad loved taking old worn-out cars and making them new again. The money was great, but the demand was few and far between, so he had to add on the other services in order to make ends meet. I remember how excited he'd get when a big restoration job would come in. He'd always take us out to dinner to celebrate the big payday. My mom would be so proud of him. They had the best relationship.

Mom was diagnosed with stage four lung cancer when I was eleven, and her health declined fast. My dad turned down jobs at the shop to focus all his attention on taking care of her and making sure there was a parent around for AJ and me. We all watched her turn frail and weak, a former shell of the beautiful woman she once was. She died later that same year and took the best pieces of us with her.

My father was a man who could literally fix anything, but

no matter what he did, he just couldn't fix her.

After that, I started helping in the office after school and on weekends, and AJ, then thirteen, went from cleanup to part-time mechanic to help lighten the load my dad suddenly had on his shoulders. Eight years later, in the wake of our dad's passing, AJ and I were once again promoted; only, this time, it was from helpers to owners.

My eyes raked over the large smoked glass ashtray that perpetually sat on my desk, the same desk that belonged to my mother. It seemed like a lifetime ago. It's been emptied and scrubbed clean, the office now a smoke-free zone, but I can't bring myself to throw it away. It sounds so silly but part of my childhood included this ashtray.

My mom was a heavy smoker. By the end of the day, the ashtray would be full of cigarette butts with tips stained red from her lipstick. My dad joked that they looked like a field of dead soldiers. My chest constricted for just a moment then, much like my mother herself, the memory was gone in an instant.

Later that night, as I was closing down the beast of a computer and preparing to leave, AJ walked into the office and plopped himself down on the couch. He looked exhausted. More exhausted than any twenty-one-year-old should look. "You okay, big brother?"

"Yeah, sis, I'm all right. It's just been a long day, and I still have a lot of work to do. I'm just happy we're getting jobs in." He lifted the brim of his trucker cap and scratched his head before setting it back down again. His dark hair curled out from underneath. He needed a haircut so bad, but who had the time? I made a mental note to learn how to cut hair on YouTube, wondering how hard it could be.

"Have you been able to get any playing in?" I knew the answer to the question already. My brother was an amazing drummer. He loved to play just as much as my dad loved his old cars.

When we were teens, I remember him banging away in various garage bands. He didn't necessarily have dreams of being a rock star, but he definitely wanted to do something musical with his life.

When mom was first diagnosed, he used to hide away in the garage of our house and bang his drums mercilessly, taking all of his aggression out on the set until he was covered in sweat and depleted of energy. Since dad died, he's barely even sat at the set at all.

"Nah. Whatever, it's kid stuff anyway." He gave a dismissive wave and rose from the couch. "I gotta get back to work. I'll see you at home."

"All right. I'll get started on dinner and give you a holler when it's done."

"Don't worry about it, just set something aside. I have a lot of work to do."

"C'mon, bro, you gotta eat. You look so tired, the work isn't going anywhere."

He blew out an exasperated sigh, grumbled something, and walked back into the shop, letting the door slam behind him.

CHAPTER TWO

Jillian

THE NEXT MORNING, same as every morning, I woke up and made my way out to the shop. The giant keyring jingled in my hand as I neared the sunshine yellow building. "Yellow stands out against the backdrop. It's bright enough to notice from the road and ridiculous enough for the customers to remember when they need to come back for more repairs," my dad had said when I asked why in God's name he'd painted the building this awful hue. At the time, it seemed silly, but now I smile, having found a new appreciation for the color.

The smell of grease in the air surrounded me, bringing me home, as I unlocked the heavy door and turned on the lights. The ancient computer churned to life with the touch of a button. It took forever to boot up making me wish, yet again, that we had money for an upgrade.

Percolating the coffee was next on my list of monotonous morning tasks. I counted out the scoops of grinds and checked the milk in the mini fridge below. A run to the store was in the near future, but there was enough to get us through the morning at least.

Once, I had complained about using this old percolator instead of a fancy Keurig machine, but AJ said it added to the charm of our business. Something about casting a nod to the olden days, much like the cars we were restoring.

A buzz overhead snapped my attention to the door just in time to see AJ come in. I had no idea what time he'd returned last night, but this morning the plate I'd left him in the microwave was empty and sitting in the sink. "Mornin', sis," he greeted me as he came over to see if the coffee was ready yet.

"Hey, you. I just put the pot on so it's going to be a few minutes. I'll bring some back when it's ready. What time did you come in last night?"

He yawned and rubbed his eye, obviously still half-asleep. "I finished up around eleven."

"AJ, you are killing yourself here. We need to hire another mechanic. You can't continue like this." I peered at my brother's weary face. He was so handsome, just like our father. He had the same dark hair and stocky build, but his eyes were light hazel, instead of my father's deep brown. He used to be such a player in his late teens. The girls would practically throw themselves at him. I couldn't remember the last time he'd been on a date. Come to think of it, I couldn't remember the last time I'd been on a date either.

I had a boyfriend once, but I'm pretty sure I was more of a conquest than anything else. As soon as he realized I wasn't ready to give him what he wanted, he dumped me fast and moved on to the next girl. I can't say I was all that upset about it either. I'd had guys ask me out between then and now, but relationships were a commodity I just didn't have the energy for. Between taking care of the shop, the house, and worrying about my brother constantly, who had time for anything else?

"We don't have the money to hire another person. People want health benefits, 401k plans, things we don't have the ability to offer. Plus, the added insurance would kill us. I'm fine. Dad handled the business, and so can I." He forgets, though, that dad *did* have help. Sporadic friends of his would come in from time to time and help him on jobs when things got busy. And, in a pinch, he always had AJ.

"I just worry about you, is all. You should be able to enjoy this time in your life. You turned twenty-one and never even went out to celebrate. You never touch your drums anymore, and even though you pretend it doesn't bother you, we both know that it does. I don't want to be a harpy, but I don't want to see you go down the same road as Dad." AJ opened his mouth to reply when the unmistakable roar of a vintage engine interrupted us. "Well, Mr. Morello, your nine a.m. just arrived."

AJ walked back into the garage to open the large bay doors as I walked around the desk to start my work for the day. Morning light cascaded through the blinds, and I caught sight of the old Ford sitting in the lot. It was a sweet car. I had to admit, I had a thing for Mustangs—especially the vintage ones. This one wasn't exactly cherry, but it was close. Its silver smoke gray paint job gleamed in the summer sunshine, and the wheels were polished and clean. Whoever owned this car loved it, and it showed. The engine purred as it idled in the lot, and AJ went out to take a look.

I was lost in my work when I heard the door buzz, alerting me that a customer had come in. My gaze was locked on the screen in front of me, crunching numbers on an Excel spreadsheet. "I'll be right with you," I muttered.

"Sure, take your time." The voice was deep and smooth, like caramel. All the tiny hairs on my arms stood to attention as my skin prickled instantaneously. I dragged my eyes away from the monitor to see who the owner of the magical sound was and was greeted by a pair of shocking green eyes and a mess of thick dirty blond hair.

My stomach somersaulted. I was sure I'd swallowed my own tongue because I could not force a word to come out of my mouth, even though I'd opened it in a valiant attempt to speak. Before I could make a bigger ass of myself, AJ walked in from the shop breaking the spell that had come over me. I tore my gaze away from the beautiful stranger, remembering that I'd promised my brother a coffee.

"Oh, I got it, AJ. Sorry, I forgot." I walked over to the percolator and started to pull the Styrofoam cups from the sleeve. Now that I was free from the confines of the enormous desk, I was able to see the customer fully. He was tall and built. His T-shirt stretched across his chest and disappeared into the unbuttoned flannel shirt he wore over it. His jeans were just tight enough to accentuate his thick legs, but not skinny jean tight like those pretty boys with their Mazda Miatas and fancy wristwatches. These were well worn as if he'd owned them forever but just couldn't get rid of them. "Can I get you something? A water, a coffee?" *A willing love slave perhaps?*

He leaned against the desk, propping himself up on his elbow, and I tried to hide the fact that I was hopelessly trying to see beyond the flannel shirt. "Sure, Jillian, a coffee'd be great." The sound of my name startled me. I creased my brows together trying to remember if I knew him from somewhere. He looked at AJ and laughed. The sound was like rain trickling on the roof at midnight, comforting and scary both at the same time. "I told you she wouldn't remember me."

My gaze darted over to my brother wondering if I was going to be let in on the big mystery, or if they were both going to continue to stand there and torture me. "It's Jameson Tate, sis. Don't you remember him? He practically lived at our house. We started that crappy garage band, and he was the guitar player."

Oh shit, I did remember Jameson Tate. Suddenly, I was transported back in time and was the same Megadeth tee-wearing tomboy sitting in our garage on a crappy old futon watching my brother and his friend attempt to recreate old heavy metal tunes. Jameson Tate was much smaller back then. Boyish and cute. There was nothing boyish about him now. The guy standing before me was definitely all man.

I remember how sweet he was, asking me if I had any requests and winking at me with that adorable lopsided grin. A lopsided grin he apparently still had, and was flashing me at this very second creating nervous feelings in the pit of my stomach. He moved abruptly from our little New Jersey town not long after he and my brother decided to start the band together. They didn't even have time to come up with a real name before he disappeared. I'm pretty sure it was going to be Rumpled Foreskin or something equally as heinous. He probably dodged a bullet by moving.

"Oh, my gosh, Jameson, of course. Wow, it's been a long time. What are you doing back in town?" I said, standing on my tiptoes to give him a hug. Was he always this tall? Being little sometimes had its disadvantages. In this case, my face squished against his collarbone instead of the crook of his neck where it should be.

"Hey, Jill, good to see you again." He wrapped his arms around my back as the sound of my name rolling off his tongue resonated in my ear. His body was solid against mine, and he smelled like soap and manliness. A rich, clean, spicy fragrance I couldn't pinpoint but didn't want to stop inhaling like smoke. As I pulled away from our quick embrace, I took another quick hit and resisted the urge to run my hands down his glorious chest.

"I came back to town a while ago to get some stuff in order. I remembered your pops had this old garage and thought I'd bring the Mustang in for an oil change. It's long past due."

The mention of my dad sent a pang into my heart. Jameson Tate must not read the obituaries very often. I went back over to the percolator and poured AJ a fresh hot cup, black, just as he liked it. *Gross.* I loved coffee, but I generally dumped enough cream and sugar in it to make it stand up on its own. "How do you like your coffee, Jame?"

"Oh, light and sweet thanks." He smiled at me again, and I noticed a little dimple on the side of his mouth. I had an overwhelming desire to run over and lick it but concentrated on fixing his coffee instead.

"That's a hot ride you got there," I said, watching the dark and light swirls dance in the coffee cup before handing it over. Our fingers grazed as he took the cup from my hand, sending shockwaves of electricity up my arm and down into my midsection.

We had stood for a few beats before AJ cut in. "I gotta get back to work, dude. It was good seeing you, though. You should come by the house one day and hang out."

Jameson blew on his hot coffee and took a sip. Never in my life did I ever wish to be a Styrofoam cup more than I did the second his lips touched that one. "You guys still live out back?"

"Yeah, we're still there. Set something up with Jill. I'll see ya later, man." AJ turned, slapping the door open with his hand and letting it slam shut behind him like usual.

The silence between us was awkward. Making small talk with regular people was hard enough, but Jameson was like a cross between an Abercrombie model and a contractor. There is nothing sexier than a hot dude with dirty hands. "Your car shouldn't take that long, so you're welcome to have a seat and hang out," I said, making my way back to my desk.

Jameson sprawled out wide legged on the couch and sipped his coffee quietly. The clacking of the keyboard was the only sound that filled the room. "So," he said, after a while. "How's the old man? I'm shocked he's not here."

I always hated this part. Morello and Son's Restoration was a well-known establishment in this town, and everyone knew my father. It wasn't uncommon for me to run into someone who would ask about my dad and what he was up to. There was no life insurance, so we weren't left with anything when he died. He was quickly cremated, and we had a small ceremony at the church.

"He died last year," I said flatly, unable to come up with an ounce of compassion. Whenever I told people my parents were dead, they always responded with that 'aww, poor you' head cocked puppy dog eyed look that made me want to throw a few punches. I didn't need anyone's patronizing sympathy.

Jameson's face showed none of that. The only look he offered up was shock. "Oh shit, I'm sorry, Jillian. I didn't know."

I put my hand up to silence his apologies, suddenly feeling guilty about blurting it out like that. "It's fine, Jame, I know. Don't worry about it." It was unfair to blow him off like that. It was a simple question, one any old friend would ask. There was a time when Jameson spent a lot of time at our house, and he got to know my dad well. They both had a love of cars, and he and my dad bonded over that similarity, something AJ had no interest in discussing with him.

"It all makes sense now," Jameson said to himself, rubbing his chin.

I looked up from the desk to hear what he had to say. "What makes sense?"

"AJ being the head mechanic, you running the office. You guys are all alone here, aren't you?"

I shrugged in response. It was just the way it was. This last year felt like an eternity, and I couldn't imagine a time when we weren't chained to this place like cogs in a dying machine.

Jameson rose from the couch and tossed his empty cup into the trash nearby. I watched from behind the desk as he walked out the front door and sat on the curb, his black and gray plaid covered forearms resting on his bent knees. He looked around.

First to one side, then the other, and then eventually just rested his head in his hands as if contemplating his next move. He stood, kicked the dirt, and disappeared through the bay doors.

Jameson

DRIVING BACK THROUGH the little town my dad forced me from was bizarre. It looked exactly the same, and it was like an instant time warp. The school, the tiny downtown strip where all of the stores were—it seemed like time had stood still in this town. I'd driven by the old yellow garage a few times since I'd been back and wondered if the Morello family still owned it. It had been five years since we spoke, but playing music and hanging out at their place was still one of my fondest memories.

Mr. Morello was a good guy. He was a hell of a lot better than the old bastard who raised me. An oil change on the Mustang was easy enough to accomplish on my own, but I figured it was worth a few bucks for the trip down memory lane. Seeing AJ working there was a surprise, and from the looks of it, he'd been there a while. Working with old cars and getting my hands dirty was always a passion of mine, and something Mr. Morello and I could talk about for hours, but AJ was different. He was really into music. I guess we all have a way of being sucked into things we never anticipated.

Seeing Jillian was even more surprising. She was the runt little sister who dressed in her dad's old oversized band tees and insisted on tagging along everywhere we went. AJ never really cared because she didn't get in the way, and it was cool with me because I kind of thought she was cute. Mr. Morello let AJ and I turn the house's detached garage into a studio of sorts so we could have a place to hang out anytime we wanted. When someone in the neighborhood was giving away a futon, we threw it in there thinking it would be a great place to bring girls. The only girl who ever actually got to use it, to my knowledge anyway, was Jillian Morello.

She would sit there for hours, just happy to watch us play and could hang as chill as any boy I knew. She said that when we made it big, she would be our roadie. I laughed at the thought of that because she was just an itty-bitty thing. She couldn't be more than five feet tall and not even one hundred pounds soaking wet.

Five years might not have done anything for the town, but it certainly did wonders for Jillian. She'd always been a pretty girl. She still had the same long brown hair and black/brown eyes, but she was definitely no runt. When she got up from that desk, I got excited to see her for completely different reasons. She was tiny in size but not in body, that was for damn sure. Her ass was fierce in those low-rise jeans, and the girl had no trouble filling out a tee shirt. She was wearing a simple Morello and Son's tee, but it was tied into a knot at the small of her back stretching the words across her ample chest. The logo practically leaped toward me in 3D. When she came in for that hug and pressed her voluptuous body against mine, my jeans suddenly felt tight.

After our little chat in the office, I stepped outside to get some air. Jillian blurting out that her father had died stirred up feelings I didn't know how to handle. Years had passed since I'd seen the man, but for some reason, I felt an overwhelming sense of loss that Mr. Morello was gone.

I remember when AJ left school because his mom died. He returned and never brought her up again. It was almost as if it never happened. My own mother died when I was just a little kid, although not exactly the same circumstances.

Cancer is sad; overdosing on prescription pain meds is just pathetic.

It was just my father and me after that, and he made it

known that my presence wasn't appreciated. I was more of a nuisance to him than anything else. Weeks would go by when he'd pretend I wasn't there at all. He'd look right through me as if I was a ghost, and then go out without ever saying a word, leaving me home alone to wonder if he'd return. He always did and always with another girl.

I use the word 'girl' because that's usually what they were. Young girls, on the brink of becoming women, but not quite there yet. Broken and sad, riddled with daddy issues they hoped my father would be able to fill.

I was too young to realize the implications of my father's actions at first. The yelling voices of my parents would echo through the walls of our tiny two-bedroom apartment, but the subject matter was lost on me. My father was a disgusting, disturbed individual.

So many nights, I stayed up wondering why my mother chose to take her own life instead of just taking me and leaving him, but I'd never have the answer to that question. My only assumption is that she feared I'd grow up just like him and couldn't bear to live long enough to see it.

All things aside, I still loved my mother, and I knew how AJ must have been feeling even though he was intent on remaining stoic about the whole thing. We bonded over the unspoken loss we both shared and became friends.

Until I was forced to leave.

AJ was standing under my car changing the oil filter as I walked back into the shop. "Hey, man, how's it going back here?"

"Just about done," he said, grabbing the greasy rag from his back pocket and wiping his hands on it.

I looked around the messy shop. All three lifts were full and there were sporadic car parts piled all over. I shoved my hands in my pockets casually. "Looks like you can use a hand."

He snorted a laugh in response. "Yeah, well, there are worse things to have than too much work, I guess. There could be none, right?"

"Jillian told me about your dad. I'm sorry, man. He was a good guy." AJ looked up from his work for a second, and I saw hurt flash in his eyes so quickly you could miss it if you weren't paying attention. "Listen, you need a mechanic and I need a job. What do you say?"

"I say that if you're looking for money, you're barking up the wrong tree. It may be busy around here but the overhead is high. There's not a lot of money left for anything else."

I nodded and let that thought sink in for a second. They were struggling. "Look, AJ. I'll do any job you have. You need the floors swept? I'm your man. You need someone to do oil changes all damn day, screw it. I'll do that too."

"I can't offer you benefits, and I'll pay you per diem, cash off the table. When there's work, I'll call ya, when there's not, I won't. Best I can offer."

"Deal. When can I start?"

AJ walked over and hit the button to lower the lift. "Come back after lunch."

CHAPTER THREE

Jillian

I HEARD THE growl of an engine in the shop and watched as AJ pulled Jameson's car out of the bay. The men stood next to it for few minutes talking, then they shook hands, and Jameson pulled away and sped out of the lot. The flicker of hurt I felt when he didn't even come in to say good-bye was silly. We weren't friends. I was just his friend's annoying kid sister who followed him around like a lovesick puppy.

He was nice eye candy for an hour, but I needed to put on my big girl panties and go about my day. As hard as I tried, however, I could not get that man out of my head. I worked the rest of that morning with the words *Jameson Tate* burning a hole on my tongue. The way his eyes danced when he saw me come away from the desk, the way his body felt as he squeezed me in that seemingly innocent hug. The office held more than the ghosts of my parents; it now included the memory of Jameson all swirling around in my head like the coffee I'd poured earlier. When lunchtime came, I couldn't wait to escape and retreat into the comfort of my home for an hour.

I called back into the garage to let AJ know I was heading out and ask him if he wanted anything. He grumbled something in response that I didn't understand, and I figured he'd just eat what I brought back.

Once upon a time, AJ was the funniest guy I knew. He would make me laugh until my sides hurt with just a stupid expression or a quick-witted joke. Now, he was so grumpy all the time that it was best to just stay out of his way.

It was hot as hell in the house. I walked around opening all the windows, opting against using the air conditioner to save on the bill before heating up some leftover pieces of the meatloaf I'd made for dinner the night prior. I put one piece on a plate for me and wrapped up another piece on a Kaiser roll for AJ.

VH1 played music videos during the day, and I couldn't help but give an appreciative little fist pump when I flipped it on and saw it was Metal Mania day. I finished my food while rocking out to classic metal tunes and prepared dinner for the evening, knowing that I hated having to do it after work. The hour went fast, and I grabbed the sandwich I'd made for AJ and headed back to the shop. Poor guy was probably famished.

I walked straight through the bay doors instead of the office and was greeted by a fine ass bent under the hood of a 1998 Ford Fiesta. This particular specimen was not sheathed in Carhart coveralls, which AJ insisted on wearing at the shop. "Can I help you with something?" The ass backed up, and two muscular arms slammed the hood down. The mystery man turned around, and the emerald green eyes of Jameson Tate greeted me.

"Jill, what's up?" I watched as he wiped his dirty hands on a nearby rag and tossed it to the side. *Oh, my gosh, he's so . . . dirty.* He'd ditched the offensive flannel shirt from earlier, and I was not disappointed seeing what he was hiding underneath it.

The sleeves of his shirt had been ripped off and were replaced by tattoos snaking up each sinewy arm. Pectoral muscles peeked out from the large openings. I stupidly held the sandwich, holding back drool, as he stood there with a thumb hooked in each armhole, his fingers threaded together in front of his thick chest. He looked at me and arched an eyebrow before turning slightly to open the car door.

"You guys need help here. I offered my services," he said answering the question I was having trouble finding the voice to ask. He placed his hand on his taut stomach when he said "services," and I couldn't stop myself from wondering what other services those hands might be skilled at performing.

I regained my composure just in time for AJ to saunter in through the bay doors. "I see you took my advice and hired some help. Thanks for sharing the good news, ass," I said, tossing him the sandwich I'd made.

"Sorry, been busy back here." He tore a piece of the tinfoil off, exposing one side and took a bite. *My brother, ladies and gentlemen, the man of many words.* He swallowed his mouthful and headed for the back of the shop, and I took that as my cue to walk away. I turned toward the office door and felt the sensation of someone at my back. The hair at the nape of my neck stood up, and my skin prickled with goose bumps again, regardless of the early June heat.

"Thanks, Jill. I promise I won't let you guys down." A colorful arm came out from behind and grabbed the handle to the office door, opening it for me. His chest lightly brushed against my back in the process causing my cheeks to flush and other areas of my body to ignite. I smiled reassuringly and walked through the door hoping he didn't realize how the simplistic move had such an effect on me.

Back at my desk, I was finding it hard to concentrate on my work for the second time that day. I needed to focus. On one hand, I was thrilled AJ finally broke down and hired some much-needed help, but on the other, I was finding it increasingly difficult to do the simplest tasks with Jameson around. The man turned me into a bumbling idiot, and I'd been in his presence for all of two minutes.

A wave of heat crested over my skin. *Is that from the temperature or something else?* I raked a hand through my long hair then twisted it, securing it with a pen that was lying on the desk.

With one quick tap of the keyboard, the bouncing screensaver disappeared and the monitor sprang to life. Staring back at me was the photo taken of my dad and me the day of my senior prom that I kept as my background. I was dressed in a long red gown with my hair swept up off my shoulders, and I remember not wanting to get the shop in the background because I was worried the yellow would clash. His eyes were wet, and he told me I looked beautiful.

Just as beautiful as my mother, he'd said.

The dark beard on his face split with an ear-to-ear grin, and his hair was combed back off his forehead. He seemed so happy and healthy in the picture. It was hard to believe that it was the last one we'd ever take together. Had I known, I might have hugged him a little tighter instead of just standing next to him, plastering on the huge fake grin and hoping my date would come soon. I swallowed the lump that was starting to form in my throat and clicked the icon for the billing software we used.

Drowning in a sea of purchase orders, I paused only to take phone calls and make appointments here and there. The majority of the afternoon flew by. I stood, stretching my arms to the sky with a yawn. My need for coffee was dire. On my way to the percolator, I caught the sight of AJ and Jameson through the window in the office door. AJ was smiling. He was actually laughing at something Jameson had said. It had been so long since I'd seen him look legitimately happy; my heart swelled with so many emotions they were hard to contain. Looking at my brother at that moment, I wondered if Jameson's sudden appearance was less coincidence and more fate. He was meant to be here.

Jameson

THE AFTERNOON AT the shop was going well. There was no shortage of shit to do, that's for damn sure. It was really cool getting to know AJ again too. He'd turned out to be a good guy, just like his dad.

It was getting close to closing time when Jillian marched out of the office. Her hair was all twisted up with a pen stuck in it. She looked like a little pixie about to blast off the ground and fly around the room. "Jameson, we're celebrating tonight. You're coming to dinner at our house, six o'clock!" She didn't ask me, she told me. Who was I to argue when a girl, especially one as cute as her, demanded I come over to her house?

I had to admit, I was more than a little eager to get to know her better. Being back here, knowing she was inside that office the whole time; it was hard for me not to go in there and just spend all day with her. It also didn't help matters that I couldn't stop wondering how easily I could probably throw that tiny girl around in my bed. The guilt I felt working alongside her brother while having these thoughts made for a very weird first day on the job.

"Go ahead and cut out for the day," AJ said, as I was pushing a broom around the floor, sweeping up metal and debris into neat piles.

"You sure, man? I can stick around and help you clean up some more."

"It's cool, man, go ahead. Besides, if you're late for dinner, my sister will kill you." He smiled and rotated his finger next to the side of his head, insinuating Jill was a little crazy. Seemed I had a thing for crazy.

"All right, dude. I'll see ya later." AJ lifted his hand up in a slight two-finger wave as I headed out the door.

Jillian crept into my thoughts the whole car ride home. There was something about her I couldn't get out of my head. The way her body fit mine perfectly when we hugged that morning. Her crisp fruity scent just daring me to take a bite to see if her skin tasted just as sweet. Her big doe eyes and tiny mouth made her appear innocent, but her body looked like it was made for sin.

Living in this dormitory sucked, but I hadn't planned to stick around, and it was non-committal. I hoped the communal bathroom was available so I could take a cold shower and suppress the half hard-on I'd been living with all day. There was no way I was walking into the Morello house sporting wood like a sex-obsessed teenager.

The room I rented was tiny. It didn't fit more than a bed, a dresser, and a lounge chair, but that was fine with me. I didn't need a lot. I stripped my dirty clothes off, kicking them into the corner to worry about later. Right then, I only had one thing on my mind—getting myself presentable and getting back to the only place I ever really felt at home.

Dinner party etiquette rules weren't part of my skill-set. My meals most nights consisted of reheated pizza or Cup O'Noodles. I watched an old movie on cable once. The man in the black and white film was telling his kid that you never show up at a girl's house empty handed. Seemed like good advice, so I opted to stop at the liquor store at the last minute to grab a bottle of wine.

The door to Jill and AJ's house was open inside, so I knocked lightly on the frame of the screen. "Come in!" Jillian called from inside. I opened the door and was immediately flooded with memories of the past.

Their house hadn't changed. The school photos of AJ and Jill still adorned all the walls in the family room, with the wedding photo of Mr. and Mrs. Morello hung strategically in the center. The floral sofa and lace curtains were exactly the way I remembered them.

I followed the worn hardwood floors to the kitchen where Jillian was standing at the counter. She'd changed her clothes since work. She had on a pair of cut-off denim shorts that hugged her ass just right. Her legs were just begging to be wrapped around someone, preferably me, and her feet were bare. Her hair had been pulled up into a neat ponytail, exposing a small star tattoo on the back of her neck.

"Hey, Jame!" She turned around to greet me, and I noticed she was wearing a faded Judas Priest tee that had been cut tank top style. The neck hung off one shoulder, and it said Exciter across the front. The shirt was autobiographical. She not only excited me, but she also lit me on fire. She came over and stood on her tiptoes to kiss me on the cheek. I bent down to match her height and inhaled her sweet fragrance as she came close. "Wine, huh? Ohh la la!" she joked, taking the bottle from my hand.

"I wasn't sure what kind you'd like. This was what the guy at the store suggested."

She read the bottle and placed it on the set dinner table. "I'm sure it's great, thank you. You didn't have to do that, though; we have plenty of beer in the fridge." She grabbed a half empty bottle of Bud from where she was standing at the counter and pressed it against her lips, tipping her head back to take a long sip. I watched her throat move as she swallowed the cold brew. When the bottle moved away from her lips, her tongue slipped between them, licking off some residual foam from the corner of her mouth. I marveled at the fact that every move this woman made was unintentionally seductive. She had no idea what she was doing to me. "You want one? Help yourself."

I walked over to the fridge to grab a beer, trying to push all the various ways I'd love to help myself to whatever she had to offer out of my mind. "Thanks. Smells delicious in here. I'm secretly thrilled you invited me to dinner. I can't remember the last time I had a good home-cooked meal." I leaned against the counter across from her and crossed my legs at the ankles.

"Well, your secret is safe with me." She winked. "Besides, don't go thanking me until after you've eaten it. Home cooking I can do, good home cooking . . ." She waved her outstretched hand from side to side in a "so-so" manner as she took another swig of her beer.

"Don't let Jill fool you. She's a great cook," AJ said, walking into the kitchen. His hair was wet like he'd just finished showering. "Hey, man, what's up?" He nodded his head back and flicked his chin up in greeting, then opened the fridge and grabbed a beer.

"'Sup," I said, repeating the salutation.

"Jeez you two, wanna take it down a notch? You're so loud, I'm getting a headache," Jill joked.

AJ snorted falling into one of the chairs at the round kitchen table. He sat hunched over, a beer resting between his thick arms looking incredibly beaten down by life. These last few years have hardened him. He was short for a dude. Hell, I'd argue that I was short for a dude. I topped out at five-foot-eleven, and he looked up to me. But small stature aside, he was built like a bear. Powerful, dense, and dark. If he was anything like he was five years ago, his loyalty ran deep, right down to the bone, but AJ was not a guy you wanted to get on the wrong side of.

I pushed myself off the counter to walk across the kitchen. "You need help with anything?"

"Nope, I'm good. The lasagna is resting; I'm just heating up some garlic bread. Have a seat." Jillian motioned to the table, and I grabbed the nearest chair.

She bent over to pull the bread out of the oven and it was

almost painful for me not to look. Her ass was like the sun. If I stared straight at it, I'd probably cry. I leaned forward on the table and turned my attention to AJ. "You still playing, man?"

He rubbed his neck and leaned back in his chair. "Yeah, I play when I can. Set's still set up in the garage. You?"

"Every now and then. I still love it but haven't had a lot of chances to play these days." That was a lie. I'd barely touched a guitar since the day I left, but I wasn't about to get into the messy details of that right now.

"I picked up an old Stratocaster at a yard sale a few years ago. Maybe after dinner, we'll head back for old time's sake." AJ tipped his beer back and drained it. Without even having to ask, Jillian came back to the table with a fresh one for him.

"You good?" she asked, pointing in my direction.

"Yeah, I'm cool. Thanks." With a nod, she turned toward the counter picking up the dish of food and bringing it back to the table. She grabbed the bread next and set it in the center, continuing her servitude, as she peeled back the tinfoil and began cutting the lasagna into squares, serving AJ first.

"Gimme your plate, Jame," she said with an upturned palm.

"Jill, sit down." I rose from the table and gingerly plucked the spatula from her hand. She quirked her brow at me as I took her plate and set a big serving on top of it before serving myself. The look on her face was one that told me she was used to this treatment. It was obvious that she'd fallen into the role of caretaker so absolutely that it was second nature at this point.

I grabbed two beers from the fridge, popped the tops, and set one in front of her before settling down in my seat again. "This looks amazing. Thank you."

CHAPTER FOUR

Jillian

"JILL, YOU REALLY out did yourself." AJ sat back in his chair and rubbed his stomach. "I'm stuffed."

"Yeah, Jill, that was the best meal I've had, probably ever," Jameson added.

My chest swelled with pride at the compliments coming from either side of the table. I knew how horribly old-fashioned it was, but my inner Italian came out big time watching the men in my life eat. After my mom had got sick, I'd taken it upon myself to prepare the meals for the family. Dad and AJ were working so hard in the shop; I figured it was the least I could do to pick up some slack.

Even if it was charred to hell, my dad always raved about whatever I made. He'd come home after a hard day and ask, "What's cookin' Paula Dean?" He never complained, always happy to come home to a hot meal regardless of what it was. "Aww shucks, guys, you sure know how to make a gal blush." I batted my eyelashes and curtsied dramatically.

I started to clear the table but Jameson stopped me. "We got this, Jill. Go take a load off." He rose from his seat and grabbed some plates from the table. AJ followed suit and carried his plate to the sink, rinsing the leftover sauce down the drain.

Sitting while the kitchen was being cleaned around me was an alien feeling. I didn't know what to do with myself. Once everything was packed up and all the dishes were in the sink, I demanded that the guys go out back, insisting I could finish loading the dishwasher myself. Once they were gone, I got to business and finished in no time.

I could hear the music emanating from the garage from the tiny kitchen window. I shoved my feet into my high tops, stuffing the laces inside like I always did, and made my way out to join the guys in the makeshift studio. The garage reminded me of another life. An old one where the only responsibility I had was keeping up my GPA while still figuring out how to party in the woods with my friends.

The door was open and the light was casting an eerie glow against the dark backdrop of night. I stopped when I saw Jameson sitting on a stool, one foot on the floor and the other on the support bar with AJ's old Strat balanced on his knee. His face was set in grim determination as he looked down at the strings he plucked with his widespread fingers. He was no Randy Rhoads, but he wasn't half-bad.

The lean muscles in his forearm rippled each time he changed his fingering on the frets. When he stopped playing, he used his pick hand to push the hair out of his face and set it behind his ear. The movement was graceful, like the music itself. He turned his head slightly and saw me watching him. A slow smile spread across his face, and my heart began to race. He raised his eyebrows knowingly. I swallowed hard, my mouth becoming dry. I was caught. I could either walk down and shake it off, or run into the house and hide like a little girl.

My feet propelled me forward, and I stepped into the garage. "Sounds good, Tate," I said, never breaking stride. I felt his eyes watching me as I walked past him and sank down onto the old futon.

"Got any requests, Jilly?" He licked his lips after he said it, inadvertently drawing attention to his mouth and making me forget that I hated being called Jilly. An intense stab of want rocketed between my legs as I imagined that tongue sliding across my body. I casually crossed my thighs and squeezed, trying to tamp down the sensation to jump off the futon and pull him back down with me. Oh, I had requests, all right. Just not ones I was willing to vocalize.

"As soon as you guys are done eye fucking each other, we can get started," AJ barked. I tore my gaze from Jameson and saw my brother glaring at him. His lids were slits and his mouth wore a frightening scowl. The look on his face was almost murderous.

My presence here was causing a disturbance in the force. I needed to get my libido in check. Jameson was an employee of ours, not my personal plaything. I jumped up from the futon, embarrassed at having been called out on my silly crush. "Whatever, dude, you don't even know what you're talking about. I'm going back inside." My stomach churned with a strange mixture of desire and fear as I ran back to the safety of the house.

What was wrong with me? I wasn't the type of girl who chased members of the opposite sex. In high school, I had girlfriends who would drape themselves over any guy who was halfway decent looking and paid them a little attention. They would spend thirty minutes in the backseat of a car, then tell me in gruesome detail the sordid events that went on there. That wasn't me. I'd fooled around a little but always hit the brakes when my suitor wanted more than I was willing to give, which was pretty much always. This sudden rush of lust was unchartered territory for me.

Jameson's presence was akin to washing your eyeglasses with Windex for the first time. You spent your whole life looking through dirty lenses, not even realizing how crisp and bright everything was until the grime was wiped away. The sudden ability to feel my own skin the second he walked into a room was terrifying. I felt drawn to him and I couldn't explain it. I only hoped it was something that worked itself out before it damaged the renewed friendship between him and AJ. My brother needed Jameson in his life more than I did.

Jameson

THE LOOK ON AJ's face when he caught me watching his sister was borderline homicidal. I'd been here less than twenty-four hours and I was already causing problems. When she got up and ran off, my first instinct was to run after her, but I kept myself planted on that stool in an effort to defuse the situation. I opened my mouth to try to melt the icy glare coming from his direction, but he spoke first. "I'm only going to say this one time, Jameson. You are welcome to hang out, and I appreciate your help at the shop, but my sister is off-limits."

"AJ, I. . . ." He put his hand up and shook his head, cutting me off.

"Jillian seems tough, but it's an act. The last thing she needs is more pain in her life when you pull another disappearing act. I'm working my ass off to pay for her school and get her the hell out of this town. She deserves better."

I ground my back teeth and nodded with understanding. He was right. Jillian deserved way better than wasting her life in a greasy old car shop. She deserved way better than me. I had nothing to offer her. I couldn't let my dick control the cognizant parts of my brain that were well aware of that fact. "Does she know why I left?"

"No, and she doesn't have to as long as you can keep it in

your pants."

"Understood."

MONDAY MORNING, I got to work just in time to see Jillian opening the office for the day. AJ's warning seared into the back of my mind most of the day yesterday, and I had to remember to play it cool.

She was still on my mind when I parked my car alongside the building and sauntered into the office. The door buzzed loudly as I entered. The coffee can she was holding slipped out of her hands sending an avalanche of tiny brown pellets all over the floor. "Shit," she cursed under her breath. "I'm not used to people being here this early." She crouched down and started scooping the grinds into a pile with her hands.

"I'm sorry. I didn't mean to scare you. Here, let me help you." I grabbed a sheet of paper from the desk and squatted down next to her, pushing the pile onto the paper like a make-shift dustpan. "It's all good." My gaze shifted from the mess to her. She was watching me from under her long, dark lashes. A lock of hair had fallen from her ponytail, and my hand moved before I had time to stop it, sliding the silky strand between my fingers and tucking it behind her delicate ear. She leaned in, brushing her cheek against my hand. I knew I should pull away, but her skin felt soft under my rough palm and I couldn't resist the urge to keep touching it.

"Mornin'." AJ pushed through the back door of the office, and I abruptly stood, taking the coffee laden sheet of paper with me and dumping it into the nearby trash. Jill looked up at me from the floor. My heart hammered in my chest at the sight of her still on her knees at my feet. She nipped at her bottom lip with her teeth, bringing my focus to her mouth, before rising up from the floor. I couldn't be sure if it was intentional or not, but it was sexy as hell and made everything that much harder. My job, my restraint, and most of all, me.

"Hey, AJ. I made a mess here with the coffee. Jameson was helping me clean it up. Gimme a few minutes to get this shit together, and I'll bring you a cup back."

"Sure, sis, no worries." Jillian turned back toward the coffeepot, and AJ walked back into the shop with me on his heels.

AJ and I worked seamlessly together most of the day, regardless of the tension in the air. I had successfully avoided Jillian, which was difficult considering she was just on the other side of the shop door, but it was better to just pretend she wasn't there than to be in her presence and fight my overwhelming need to feel her smooth skin again. Keeping her off my mind, however, was not as easy. The memory of her face as she looked up from her position on the floor assaulted my mind all morning. Her lips were shiny with fresh gloss, and I imagined the various flavors that would await me should I ever be lucky enough to have her full lips against mine. As if I conjured her out of thin air, she appeared in the shop.

"You guys hungry?" She sauntered over with two individual Tupperware containers full of leftovers for us. She gave me a heated look as I took the warm container from her tiny hand, suddenly ravenous although lasagna wasn't exactly what I had in mind.

I'd been around and have had my fair share of women. I wasn't pulling Charlie Sheen numbers or anything, but I'd done all right. Some of them I was into, others I wasn't, but none of them made me feel the same energy as Jillian did. It was strange. She didn't just wreak havoc on my hormones, but she messed with my mind as well. I found myself thinking about the weirdest shit, like what her favorite band or her favorite color was. The sing-song way she said my name would pop into my mind at random times throughout the day. It slid through her teeth like she wanted to hold onto it just a little bit longer before letting it out.

The temptation of the forbidden fruit was a definite possibility, but I couldn't help but feel like it was more than that. Only time would tell if that feeling was real or fantasy.

CHAPTER FIVE

Jillian

AJ AND JAMESON both washed up, and then retreated to the office to eat their lunch on the couch. "You guys got plans for Fourth of July weekend?" Jameson asked between bites of food.

"Nah, not really. Gonna close up the shop. Looking forward to the time off," AJ replied.

"Oh, yeah? That should be cool. You know, I heard Megadeth is playing at the Arts Center. Lawn seats are probably cheap as hell. We should go." My ears perked up like a puppy, and my stomach coiled with excitement. Megadeth was my absolute favorite band. My dad took AJ and me to a concert in the city once a few years ago, and I'd love to see them again.

On the surface, my dad seemed like a normal guy, but his love of heavy metal turned him into a head banging hard rock fanatic. He dragged us to every concert he could, as soon as he felt we were old enough to handle the crowd. I guess you could say rock music was in our blood.

"I don't know, man. Driving down the shore on Fourth of July weekend sounds like a nightmare."

"AJ, live a little. C'mon, it will be a blast!" I hated the desperate sound of my own voice as I begged my brother for a night out. He needed a fun weekend just as badly as I did, if not more. I grabbed my phone and scrolled through my song list until I found the one I was looking for. The raunchy growl of Dave Mustaine filled the small office. AJ rolled his eyes, but I knew I'd convinced him.

"All right, we'll go. Go online and grab some tickets and find a hotel. May as well stay overnight."

I did a little happy dance in my seat and swung back to the computer to check out Ticketmaster. An overnight stay down the shore sounded amazing, but the thought of sleeping in such tight quarters with Jameson awakened the kind of smutty thoughts you only read about in trashy romance novels. I didn't have a lot of physical experience, but I had an imagination that could make a sailor blush. I was almost grateful that AJ would be with us so I didn't make a complete fool of myself.

AJ finished the rest of his lunch and dropped the soiled dish on the desk, knowing I'd wash it for him later. "Thanks for lunch, sis," he said with an appreciative little head pat. I shooed him away and he headed out through the back door of the office wearing a goofy grin.

Jameson popped the lid back on his Tupperware and stood, stretching his long body up to the ceiling. I watched his muscles flex as he reached for the sky, catching a glimpse of his firm stomach as his shirt rose. Well-worn jeans hung so low on his hips that the band of his boxers peeked out from underneath. A trim little happy trail disappeared beneath them, and I suddenly knew how the silly stream of hair got its name. The sight didn't just make me happy; I was downright ecstatic. He was all lean muscle, ink, and grease wrapped up into one tantalizing package that I wanted to unwrap. Slowly.

He groaned releasing the tension in his stretch and my body shuddered. The sound was like heaven, and I wanted to hear more of it, preferably coming from my bedroom. I was starting to feel like a head case.

"Jill?"

The sound of my name brought me back from la la land and snapped me back to attention. "I'm sorry, what?" I felt like a dumbass. *He's trying to talk to me, but I'm too busy drooling on my desk to notice.*

Jameson flashed a wry grin. *Yeah, he totally caught me checking him out.* "What should I do with this?" he said, holding up the empty bowl.

"Oh, uh, just leave it here next to AJ's. I'll take care of it." I pointed to the corner of my desk where AJ had dropped his just a few moments prior.

Jameson walked around the desk and placed the bowl next to the other one. The combination of oil, spice, and laundry detergent tingled in my nostrils as he leaned over my shoulders. Muscular arms came from behind me, and his hands rested on the arms of the chair. "Thanks, Jill. It was delicious."

The deep timbre of his voice tickled my ear, and my palms grew damp. His fingertips grazed up my arm as he stood again, trailing across the nape of my neck and causing chills to break out over my skin. I heard the shop door slap, and I blew out the breath I'd been holding since I felt him get close.

His erratic behavior was maddening. He was a mix between sweet and aloof, with some sexual undertones added in for flavor. I had no clue what to make of all of it. Did he feel the same instant connection I did the minute he entered the room, or was it just a game to see how many shades of pink he could turn my cheeks?

Three days ago, my life was simple, albeit boring, but at least, I didn't have these burning questions on my mind and between my thighs keeping me awake at night.

Every time I closed my eyes, images of Jameson Tate touching me in ways no man ever had flashed through my mind. His lips devouring mine and his hands caressing my body all over.

Part of me wondered what would happen if I acted on my impulses and told him these secret desires. Would one night with him quench my thirst, allowing me to return to my normal state of mind?

I sighed restlessly knowing I'd never know the answers to these questions because I was too much of a coward to ever tell him about the power he had over me.

THE DEEP RUMBLING of the engine could be heard a split second before the car appeared, and I knew Jameson had arrived. I'd confirmed the motel reservations, and double and triple checked that I had the concert tickets in my bag. The weekend of the concert was finally here, and I was so excited I felt like I could burst.

As the weeks flew by, Jameson proved himself to be a great asset around the shop. He was an excellent mechanic and wasn't afraid to get his hands dirty. The three of us developed a flawless working relationship. I'd take the orders and they'd fill them.

AJ hadn't said much about it, but I knew he was looking forward to the concert as much as I was. As the days grew nearer, he seemed easier to smile, joking around almost like he once did. I even heard him from the hallway, warbling a hatchet job rendition of "Sweating Bullets" in the shower the other day. Having Jameson at the shop wasn't only having an effect on me, but it was making a marked improvement on AJ's attitude as well. He was less broody than he was before. He would never admit it, but he was happy Jameson had returned.

"AJ, let's go!" I called out as Jameson's car appeared in front of our house. I grabbed my backpack and walked out the door to greet him. He stepped out of his car when he saw me emerge from the house, a huge smile plastered on his beautiful face. "Holy hell, that shirt rules!" Written across his broad chest were the words *This One Goes to Eleven*. I laughed at the *This Is Spinal Tap* movie reference that most people our age would never understand. It was an unspoken bond shared by only us.

I slid into the red leather bucket seat of the Mustang and checked out the interior. It was original except for the CD player added under the dash. The smell of exhaust and Jameson washed over me as I breathed deep, a combination that was both vintage and new at the same time and was quickly becoming my favorite fragrance.

AJ crawled into the expansive backseat, tipping his hat over his face and sprawling out like he was in a five-star hotel, and Jameson slipped into the driver's side right after. "You ready kids?!" he said, rubbing his hands together. His childlike excitement made me grin.

"What kind of tunes do you have in here?" I grabbed the CD book, and the shiny silver discs glinted in the sunlight as I flipped through pages. Funny how even now something as modern as compact discs seemed retro when compared to iPods and flash drives. I briefly considered vocalizing that concept but decided against it.

I pulled out a disc and popped it into the slender opening of the CD player. The car filled with heavy drumbeats and loud ruckus guitar playing and I nodded along. Jameson began to sing under his breath, subconsciously playing air guitar on the steering wheel. I kicked off my shoes and put my feet up on the dash. For the first time since I could remember, I felt young and free.

The idea of being nineteen in a house with no parents breathing down your neck was highly overrated. On the contrary, AJ and I in that big house without them was lonely. All of that space was suffocating.

Their bedroom door remained closed. Neither of us

ventured that far down the hall. It was almost as if we were scared. Death awaited all who entered. Instead, we just went about our business pretending this was normal behavior.

I'd never complain, though. Every day I was thankful that our parents left us with a roof over our heads and a steady source of income. We were incredibly lucky and much better off than many other people would be in our situation, but that didn't change the fact that I missed out on being young. All my friends scattered to the colleges of choice, pledged sororities, and waved their little pom-poms at Homecoming while I managed a broken-down auto shop and took care of my damaged older brother. I would never change it, but it was nice to be able to escape it for a while.

Jameson

I LOVED MY car. I used the word love—the emotion that trumps all other emotions, the end all be all of feelings—to describe that vehicle. I loved it as a mother loves her baby, as a yuppie loves money, as most of Texas loves Jesus. I never realized, though, how intensified that love could get until Jillian Morello was sitting shotgun inside of it.

My gaze kept shifting her way from the corner of my eye. She was stretched out on the seat like it was designed specifically for her. Her arms were up over her head and draped over the back of the seat, her bare legs curved up toward the dash. Her child-size feet bopped along with the beat coming from the speakers and, fuck me, she'd painted her toenails pink. It was so unlike her, but something about that color against her skin drove me nuts. My brain started contemplating the other parts of her that might be that same shade, and my dick jerked in my pants. I was probably going to run off the road and kill us all, but I couldn't stop peeking over to check her out.

The Arts Center was packed even though we arrived with plenty of time to spare. We drank beer and listened to CDs until it was time to go in. Jillian wasn't technically old enough to drink but that didn't make a difference to me. I could tell by her cute little giggle that she had a nice buzz going as we walked up the steep hill to get to the top of the grassy area.

The opening act started shortly after we had laid our blanket on the grass. They were a local band I hadn't heard before. While they seemed pretty decent, I didn't really pay that close attention. As soon as Jillian started to dance, everything else stopped.

She was swaying her hips back and forth to the rhythm of the music and shaking her sweet ass. I stealthily readjusted myself, hoping like hell AJ didn't catch a glimpse of me eyeballing his sister. I felt guilty, as if I was somehow betraying him, but I convinced myself looking was not the same as touching. A technicality, but hell, it worked for me.

The concert was amazing; Megadeth kicked major ass. We raised our lighters in memory of Mr. Morello during "A Tout le Monde," and when the bass line for "Peace Sells" suddenly started right after, the three of us lost our minds. By the end of the show, we were screaming along with every song and pumping our fists in unison.

The after-show buzz carried us down the hill when the show was over. Jillian's midnight hair blew in the evening breeze as she and AJ walked a few steps ahead. I just hung back as they discussed the show, watching in awe at the way they interacted with each other.

There was this stereotype I heard once that Italians talk with their hands. Jillian talked using her whole body. She was always so animated, and her excitement was infectious. I'd never seen anyone come alive quite the same way she did.

AJ listened, a look of adoration on his face, as his sister went on about Dave Mustaine's vocals and how getting booted out of Metallica was the best thing to ever happen to heavy metal. The bond between them was so unique. When we were kids, wherever AJ went was where Jillian wanted to be. I didn't have many memories of AJ that didn't include her. She was his shadow. He never fought it or told her to get a life. He genuinely liked having her around. I was happy they had each other. I knew first hand that having no one sucked.

Jill was shivering by the time we got to the car. "You cold?"

"A little bit." She was wearing a tank top and shorts. It hadn't occurred to me how much the temperature had dropped since we'd arrived earlier that day. I grabbed my sweatshirt from the backseat and hung it over her shoulders. It was huge on her, but damn, she looked adorable in it. It was a contrast to the kickass tough chick who was banging her head like a beast just a short time ago. I zipped up the front, rubbing her arms to seal in the warmth.

"How's that, cutie?"

"Better," she said, with a sigh and a smile. I held the door open as she got in the car, then slammed it shut and ran around to my own side.

By the time we made it back to the motel, AJ had already sacked out in the backseat. It was clear he was exhausted, but Jillian seemed like she was getting a second wind. "I'm beat, guys. I'm heading up. You coming or what?" AJ said, stretching his legs in the parking lot.

Jillian's stomach made a noise. "I'm actually hungry. You wanna come to the boardwalk with me and get some pizza?"

"Yeah, I'll go. AJ, you want us to bring you something back?"

"Nah, you go ahead. I'll see ya guys in a bit." AJ turned and started up the steps to the second-floor motel room the three of us were sharing for the night. He was leaving us alone together. That might not seem like a big deal, but for AJ, it was huge. The guy was quiet, almost like he was lost in his own head, but he wasn't. He silently watched, taking in everything around him. I'd earned his trust and there was no way I was going to break it.

I turned back to Jillian. "Let's do it," I said.

CHAPTER SIX

Jillian

JAMESON AND I headed toward the boardwalk side by side, our arms brushing together as we walked. The air was crisp and salty from the ocean, and the smell of food wafted from the boardwalk as we approached. Carnival rides spun in the distance, people weaved around us laughing and talking, pushing baby carriages, carrying enormous stuffed prizes, or eating the various delicacies that only the Jersey Shore offered. We made it to Jenks and found an empty table. "I'll go up. What do you want?" he asked me.

"Um, just a slice and a Coke. Thanks!"

"Okay, I'll be right back. Don't go anywhere," he said with a wink, flashing me his adorable lopsided smirk. I didn't bother to mention that I had no intention of leaving. The only place I wanted to be was wherever he was.

As soon as I was out of his line of sight, I brought his sweatshirt up to my nose and inhaled deeply. The clean smell of Jameson surrounding me was more warming than the jacket itself.

He came back to the table balancing the pizza and drinks in his large hands and set everything down between us. I pushed up the sleeves on the oversized jacket, refusing to take it off even though I was feeling much warmer, but they kept slipping as I tried to eat. His long fingers wrapped gently around my wrist. "Here, let me," he said, rolling the sleeve of the sweatshirt up, then extending his palm for my other arm. "There, how's that?"

I nodded my head; the fact that he was still holding my hand not lost on me. His calloused thumb moved in a small circular motion along my palm sending an army of tingles up my arm. His sea green eyes landed on mine. Was he looking for approval? If so, he had it. It didn't matter what he wanted; my answer was always yes.

The pizza in front of me was a lot less interesting than it was two minutes prior. My eyes silently dared him to make a move, to say something, to do anything. I breathed deep and chewed my bottom lip hoping this moment between us lasted. He stared hard at my mouth, then his gaze dropped to the steady rise and fall of my chest.

Something I couldn't quite place flashed across his face. He tore his eyes away and dropped my hand. "We should start getting back." He rose from the table and threw his empty plate in the trash nearby, leaving me sitting breathless and wondering what I did wrong.

Jameson walked ahead of me on the way back to the motel, his hands shoved firmly into his pockets not saying a word about our almost moment. I was practically running to keep up with him, his long strides taking up much more ground than my short ones. "Jameson, wait!" I shouted. He stopped and paused a beat before turning to face me. "Why are you running from me?" I caught up to him and stood catching my breath. "Do you want to explain to me what the hell that was all about?"

"What *what* was about?" he asked, a look of surprise shadowing his face.

Was he serious? This hot-cold BS was starting to get a little old. "Are you screwing with me?" I threw my hands up and let them drop at my sides.

He looked at me like I was crazy. "Is that what you think I'm doing, Jillian?" He cocked his head to the side as he continued. "Do you feel screwed with?" His taunting manner made me switch from wanting to mount him to wanting to scratch his eyes out.

I looked at him through narrowed slits. His sarcasm was not appreciated. "Go to hell, Jameson. Better yet, just go fuck yourself." I stormed past him down the length of the boardwalk. I heard his heavy footsteps coming closer to me and knew there was no way I could outrun him.

"Jillian, stop!" He grabbed my arm, and I slowed my pace. "Look, I'm sorry. I'm a dick, okay? I'm just . . . tired. Let's just go back to the motel and forget this happened. Please?" His eyes softened. They were begging me for forgiveness for whatever was going on inside that head of his.

I rolled my eyes and blew out an exasperated huff. "All right, dick, let's go."

Jameson

I HONESTLY HAD no idea why I was picking a fight with Jillian at that exact moment. *Like I said, I'm a dick.* It was just so much easier to have her mad at me than to try to explain my messed-up reasoning for the way I was acting. I had no control over myself when she was around, and it was becoming more obvious day by day. When she told me to go fuck myself and stormed away, I was both shocked and aroused. Ridiculous, I know, but hearing such dirty words from such a sweet little mouth was sexy as hell. It was clear she wasn't going to take any of my shit, and that kind of confidence was a major turn-on. I was pretty sure I'd met my match.

Jillian Morello had no problem handing my ass back to me.

The walk back to the motel was somewhat tense, but she was talking to me so that was a bonus. By the time we reached the place, I was sure our stupid spat was forgotten. We walked up the stairs to the second-floor single file. She reached the door first, swiping the stupid key card thing they gave us in the office and stepping into the room. I bumped her from behind when she stopped short. "Do you smell that?" she asked looking around and sniffing at the air.

I gave a little sniff but didn't notice anything weird. "What am I supposed to be smelling?"

"It smells like smoke." She followed her wrinkled up nose, walking deeper into the room smelling the air as she went. A gasp floated out of her. She stood at the glass slider at the back of the motel like a gaping statue before screaming, her Minnie Mouse voice going up, at least, three octaves. "What. The. *Fuck* are you doing?" she yelled. I ran over to see what the deal was just in time to see AJ flick a cigarette butt over the railing.

Her bottom lip quivered as she stood there dumbfounded. Her face volleyed between sheer fury and pure terror. AJ closed his eyes and inhaled deeply before speaking. "Jillian, don't freak out." He stepped toward the screen door like he was approaching a rattlesnake.

"How could you?" she whispered, her eyes brimming with tears. AJ slid the screen door open and reached out for his sister. Her mouth screwed up into a tiny knot and her eyes narrowed. *"How could you?"* she screamed.

AJ winced and pulled back. Tears cascaded down Jillian's face as she backed into the room, trying to escape her brother like he was a bomb. I stayed off to the side, backed against the wall, as AJ came fully into the room. "Jillian, relax. Breathe, it's okay."

"It's not fucking okay!" she gasped between sobs, picking up AJ's shoe from the ground and hurling it in his direction. He swerved, and it hit the wall with a loud thud. "Don't you remember . . ." Another shoe flew, and AJ swerved again. " . . . how horrible it was . . ." One of the complimentary cups set out on the desk flung toward AJ next. This one hit him in the chest and bounced off. " . . . to watch her die?" She tripped over a backpack and collapsed hard onto her ass. Deflated and defeated, she crumpled into a ball sobbing on the floor, her face soaked and her nose running.

AJ tentatively walked over and knelt on the floor, wrapping his arms around her. He looked up at me to gauge my reaction, but I just stood there, stunned at what I had just witnessed.

"I remember Jill, I remember," he said to her over and over as he held her to his chest and stroked her hair. She mumbled something I couldn't quite make out. AJ must have missed it too because he pulled her away and wiped her tears with his thumbs. "What was that?"

Jillian looked up at AJ with sad eyes, calming down just enough to repeat herself. "Why do you want to leave me too?" She crumpled again after the words left her mouth, and AJ squeezed her tighter.

"I'm never going to leave you, Jill. I promise I'm never leaving." He rocked from side to side rubbing her back until her breathing started to regulate. She'd completely cried herself out.

AJ was stuck on the floor, his sister curled in his lap. I lifted her up and placed her in one of the beds. Her sleeping body eked out a few stuttering breaths, but she relaxed again, and AJ and I went outside to talk.

"I've never seen a girl lose her shit like that. You wanna explain to me what the hell that was about?"

AJ wiped a hand down his face, his Zildjian T-shirt wet from

Jillian's tears. "Remember I told you our mom died from cancer?" I nodded. "It was lung cancer from smoking."

I leaned against the balcony and scratched my head thoughtfully, my arms crossed over my chest and lips sucked into a thin line as I processed what he just told me. "What is wrong with you, man?" I finally asked.

He plopped into one of the balcony chairs and dropped his head into his hands, pushing his hair out of his face. "I know how terrible it looks, believe me, but, Jameson, the stress is killing me. My dad died and everything fell to me to take care of. I put everything aside to finish the life that he started, and I never wanted any of this." He shoved his knuckle in his eye and continued. "But I can't sit back and be a selfish prick and watch his legacy die. If the business goes, then there's nothing left of the Morello family and everything my dad worked so hard for was for nothing."

"That's not true, bro. You and Jillian *are* the Morello family. Whether you're fixing cars or playing music or dancing a jig, you'll always be the Morello family. Your dad's legacy lives through you. Your occupation is irrelevant," I said sitting in the chair next to my friend.

"You just don't get it, bro," he said quietly. "The sign on the door says Morello and *Son*'s. I wasn't given the opportunity to choose." He stood up and walked into the room leaving me sitting outside alone.

CHAPTER SEVEN

Jillian

I WOKE UP and looked around. It was dusk outside and the room was still dark, but a nearby streetlight cast a sliver of light in through the balcony door, just enough that I could see my surroundings. AJ laid in the bed next to mine, his chest rising and falling with each sleeping breath. Jameson was asleep on the floor between us. I sat up and kicked my feet over the side of the bed, then knelt down on the floor beside him. "Jameson," I whispered shaking him from his sleep. His eyes fluttered open and he looked up at me. "What are you doing on the floor?"

"Well, I wasn't about to crawl into bed and spoon AJ," he whispered back. I smiled at his joke.

"C'mon, come lie with me," I said, giving his arm a gentle tug.

He swallowed hard. "No, I'm fine on the floor. You go ahead back to bed."

"Don't be an ass. Just get up here." I climbed back into bed, tossing the corner of the blanket back, an invitation for him to join me. He rose from the floor and crawled in next to me. We laid on our backs under the blanket, silently staring up at the ceiling, the moment feeling more awkward than I anticipated. My hand moved from my chest to my side and rested against his. "Jameson?" I said quietly.

"Mmmhmm."

"I'm sorry about earlier. You shouldn't have had to see that." AJ and I watched our mother turn from a vibrant young woman to a frail skeleton almost overnight, brought on by her own disgusting habit. I didn't know when he started or how he managed to hide it from me, but watching him make the conscious decision to travel down the same path was something I never expected. I lost my shit, and I was embarrassed that Jameson was there to witness it.

He turned his head to look at me, only the outline of his face visible in the dark. "You never have to apologize to me, Jillian."

I rolled to my side snuggling against him. His arm slid under me pulling me into his chest and wrapping around my shoulder. His body was warm and his heartbeat thrummed rhythmically in my ear lulling me back to sleep.

SOMEONE IN THE room was clearing their throat. I ignored it, snuggling into the bed and pulling the covers up around me. I heard it again, louder and more abrasive this time. I peeked through one eye to find AJ, leaning against the doorframe of the bathroom, arms crossed over his chest watching me sleep. *Creepy much?* The warm body against my back shifted, and the arm wrapped around my middle tightened, sliding a hand between my ribs and the mattress.

Jameson.

"Comfortable?" he asked with a raised eyebrow. The scowl on his face said all that needed to be said. Jameson and I in bed together was crossing some imaginary line he drew in the sand, but based on my big discovery last night, I knew he wasn't going to say a damn thing about it. Besides, we were both fully dressed. It was obvious nothing happened.

I pushed myself up on my elbow, the vibrant arm still locked tightly around my waist. "What time is it?"

"It's nine thirty. Check out is at eleven, so if you wanted to take a shower or something, I suggest you do it now." He walked over to his bed and grabbed his wallet shoving it into the back pocket of his shorts. Jameson looked so peaceful sleeping next to me. A long piece of hair curled around his cheekbone creating a tawny frame around his closed eye. My fingers twitched, desperately wanting to run through it, but I held them at bay. Instead, I peeled his arm back and slipped out of bed making sure I didn't disturb him. The ride back was long, and I wanted to let him sleep. "I'm going to run down and grab us some coffees. I'll be back," AJ added. The door clicked behind him, and he was gone.

The water sputtered out of the showerhead before shooting out hot and sharp on my skin. Waking up in Jameson's arms was surreal. His breath on my neck and his warm body pressed against mine, I wanted to stay in that bed with him forever to just be held.

The feeling of his arm secured around me still tingled across my middle like a missing limb, as I finished my shower and stepped out. His skin was soft, which was a complete contrast to the roughness of his hands. Hands I couldn't stop imagining all over me, as I rubbed my body dry with the sandpaper motel towel. I reached for the pile of clothes I'd thrown onto the toilet seat. Of course, I'd forgotten my underwear. It crossed my mind to put the ones from yesterday back on, but I decided that was gross.

Just slip out, get what you need, and sneak back in.

With the towel wrapped tighter around myself, I opened the door. The bed we shared was a tangled mess of empty blankets. I felt eyes boring into me from the corner of the room, like a laser beam burning a hole clear through my body. My gaze traveled the length of the brilliant green beam into eyes of the same color.

"Jill," Jameson said, greeting me. It was only one word, a fragment really, four little letters sliding off his tongue slithering around me like his inked up arm was not that long ago.

No other words were spoken after that. We stood on opposite ends of the room staring each other down. My eyes traced the lean lines of his shirtless, beautiful body. Tattoos popped off the backdrop of his skin. Flawless, smooth, and tan all over, no doubt from working outside in the sun, his torso was a perfect letter V, from his broad shoulders to his slim waist. I imagined running my hands across the hard plane of his abs following the trail of muscles that disappeared beneath his jeans. I'd heard them called so many different things, but the pathway to heaven seemed like the ideal name to describe them now.

Jameson's eyes narrowed on the towel as if he was looking through it with X-ray vision. My hand sprang to the knot at my chest. Whether I was holding it tighter or preparing to tear it away in a sacrificial offering, I wasn't sure. My heart pounded in my ears. The silence between us was deafening. I opened my mouth to say something, anything to break the sweltering tension, when I heard the door accept AJ's key card. Jameson's eyes flicked toward it and back at me. He wet his lips with his tongue and turned away. I backed into the bathroom and closed the door behind me. *Maybe I don't need underwear today.*

Jameson

I FELT THE cold instantly the moment her body left mine. The sound of running water gave off the illusion of rain outside. Reaching for her, I found nothing but vacant sheets. The room was empty.

Getting into bed with her was dangerous ground but when she climbed in and looked at me, her eyes pleading with me to come with her, she still looked so friggin' sad. It took every ounce of willpower I had not to roll her over and pin her to the mattress under me until she was crying out in pleasure instead of pain.

Her tiny body curled up next to mine like we were puzzle pieces that were meant to fit together. I held her closer than I had the right to. The fruity scent of her hair drove me nuts. It got inside my brain and wreaked havoc on my dreams. She was just a girl, like dozens of others I've had in my bed except . . . she wasn't. Jillian wasn't just any girl; she was *the* girl. The proverbial unicorn—ideal in every way yet unattainable.

If AJ caught us in bed together, he'd be pissed. At some point, I'd have to sit him down and assure him that nothing happened between Jillian and me, to reassure him that nothing would happen. I thought about how to broach the subject as I was getting dressed. When the bathroom door opened, any residual thoughts I'd had about AJ disappeared.

She stood there wearing nothing but a towel, her wet hair falling over her slender shoulders leaving tiny droplets of water on the crappy beige carpet at her feet. She looked surprised to see me at first, but then her surprise turned into something else.

The look in her eyes was carnal. Her hands clutched the towel, holding it tighter around her and making it easier to see the outline of her body from under its bulk. It only made me want to run over there and tug it away, to lick off the droplets of water that had collected around her chest and shoulders and make her mine like I pretended she was last night.

The thought was fleeting. As quickly as she appeared,

she disappeared and AJ came into the room holding a tray of Styrofoam cups. "Hey Jame, I got us some coffees for the ride home."

I quickly threw on the shirt I'd been mangling in my fist and took the coffee from AJ's hand. "Thanks, man," I said, taking a sip and turning my back to him. How could I look the guy in the face while imagining the many ways I wanted to defile his sister in that exact moment? *Man, I really am such an asshole.*

The bathroom door opened, and I heard her feet padding out onto the carpet. "Oh, Jameson, you're up," she said. I was confused. For a minute, I thought I'd imagined the whole thing. That maybe I was still in bed holding her in my arms and this was just a weird vivid dream I was having.

I glanced in her direction. She was standing behind AJ. The crimson flush on her cheeks assured me that I was wrong. She was ignoring it—pretending it didn't happen—either for AJ's sake or her own.

"Yeah," was all I said as I grabbed my toothbrush and locked myself in the bathroom. My fingers curled over the edge of the sink. "Get it together, man," I said to my own reflection. I scratched at the stubble on my jaw and thought about shaving but decided against it. We needed to get out of the confines of this room as quickly as possible, but I didn't want to take her home yet. Last night was a clusterfuck of epic proportions, and I couldn't have that be the last thing she remembered about this weekend. I wanted to spend more time with her. I wanted to spend all my time with her. As I brushed my teeth, I tried to think of something to say to prolong our short weekend together.

The room beyond the bathroom door was quiet. Jillian was sitting cross-legged on the bed we shared, her coffee resting between her legs as she scrolled through her phone. She looked up at me with the same carnal look in her eyes as I entered the room, only this time I refused to look. I didn't have to. It devoured me whole as I stood there pretending she didn't affect me in the slightest. "You guys ready to go?" AJ said hiking his backpack up on his shoulder. I wasn't, but I nodded my head and grabbed my stuff anyway.

The ride home was tense. The energy in the car that was so vibrant yesterday had returned to the same bleak black and gray it was a few weeks ago when I'd started at Morello's.

As we pulled in front of the house, I felt my chest tighten. I didn't want to see her go. I wanted her to wake up in my arms every morning and fall asleep next to me every night. My feelings for her had gotten so strong in just a few weeks, and I couldn't figure out what it was about her that was drawing me in. Sure, she was hot, but it was more than that. The connection to her was like nothing I'd felt before with anyone else. She had an energy around her, a force field. The more I fought it, the harder I felt the pull. I intended to keep my promise to AJ, but when she was around, everything about my shit life seemed better. She was my rainbow in the dark.

"That was a lot of fun, Jameson. Thanks," she said. She opened the car door and jumped out, pushing the seat forward for AJ. My mind raced as I thought of ways to keep her from going back in the house.

"Jill, hold up!" I got out of the car and stood in her drive. She and AJ both turned to look at me.

Think of something, dude.

"Do you know how to cut hair?" The second it flew out of my mouth, I wanted to groan. What the hell was I even talking about? I sounded like an idiot.

"Um," she started, using her pinky to tuck her hair behind her ear and twirling the end around her finger. "I cut AJ's hair recently. I wouldn't say that I really know what I'm doing, though."

"Oh. Well, that's okay. I was just thinking, you know, since I'm here and all. My hair is getting kind of long."

Stupid. Stupid. Stupid.

"Okay, well, come on in, and I'll see what I can do." She turned and walked toward the house. I slammed my door and followed her in. Truth be told, my hair was shaggy as hell, but I kind of liked it that way.

"Lemme go grab the clippers." She ran up the stairs leaving me waiting in the hall.

"Good luck, man," said AJ with a grin as he walked past me to get to the stairs. "It's no coincidence I always wear a hat."

Jillian came down the stairs with a tackle box looking thing in one hand and a towel in the other. "Let's go out back. That way there isn't hair all over the house." I followed her out and sat in the lawn chair she'd set out for me. She wrapped the towel over my shoulders like a cape, held it with a hair clip in the front, and then took a comb from the box. My eyes almost rolled back into my head when she raked the comb gently through my hair. Holy shit, it felt good. "How do you want it?"

The innocent question made my dick spring to life. My first thought was *from behind,* but I wiped that shit from my mind real quick. "Just a trim, I guess. Don't buzz me or anything."

Her giggle sounded like wind chimes. "I won't, don't worry." My body lit up like a Christmas tree as her fingertips grazed the back of my neck and my ears. I'd never found a task as simple as this so erotic, but her touch did things to me I couldn't quite explain.

"Now, sit still." She cut the back first then came around to do the front, combing the hair toward my face. I could feel her warmth on my thigh, hot and humid, as she straddled my leg between hers, practically sitting on top of me. My erection pressed against my fly making it hard to think. I balled my hands on my lap to keep from grabbing her ass and pulling her in.

She moved to the other side and switched up the legs, throwing the scissors on the table when she was done. They skidded across the tempered glass and clanged onto the concrete, but she didn't move from my lap. Instead, she leaned in, pressing against my chest and allowing the hair to slip between her fingers as I inhaled my favorite smell in the whole world. She used her nails to scratch my scalp as she pushed all the hair back off my face. Her lips were so close to mine. All it would take was one small move, a tiny blip in the Earth's rotation, to close the space between us.

"I think I'm done. Do you wanna go see?" She took the towel from my shoulders and swept some residual hair away. A few stragglers remained. Every nerve in my body danced as her warm breath rolled across my neck in her attempt to blow them off.

"Nah, it's cool. I trust you," I said touching the tingling sensation on the back of my neck. "Thanks a lot, Jill. I appreciate it."

"No problem. You want a beer?" My heart smiled at her offer. I took that as a clue that she wanted me to stay just as badly as I wanted to.

"I'd love one," I replied and followed her into the house.

CHAPTER EIGHT

Jillian

CUTTING JAMESON'S HAIR made me nervous. It wasn't just that I was afraid I'd mess it up, which I was, but being that close to him made the butterflies in my stomach feel like Olympic gymnasts.

His hair felt like silk sliding between my fingers, and he made the faintest moaning noise that turned my legs to jelly. I didn't have to get as close to him as I did but I wanted to. I wanted to sit down on his lap and grind away the pulsating ache between my thighs that was distracting me. It was just a stupid haircut, but I loved that he asked me to do it.

He followed me into the house, and I grabbed two beers from the fridge and handed them to him. "Let me go grab some music and meet you back outside." I ran up the stairs and poked my head in AJ's room. "I'm done with Jameson's hair. You wanna come down and hang out?"

"Nah, I'm gonna head to the shop and check on things. I'll be back in a bit."

"Suit yourself." I started to walk away, but he called me back.

"Last night was a disaster and I'm sorry. You're absolutely right, and I'm going to stop, okay?"

I swallowed hard trying not to get upset all over again. "Then I guess I'm sorry I threw your shoes," I replied with a smile,

"That's all right. Your aim is terrible." He laughed.

I snorted at his joke then became more serious. "Thanks, AJ. It means a lot to me." He nodded, and I went into my room to grab what I sought out and returned to Jameson on the patio. He'd swept up the hair remnants and wiped down the table for me. "Well, Mr. Tate, aren't we just so domesticated?"

A wry grin flashed across his face. "I checked out my hair while you were upstairs. I'm a sexy motherfucker, too."

Hell yeah, you are.

I plugged my phone into the dock and set it on auto play. Loud, nasty guitar riffs came blasting out of the tiny purple speaker followed by Vince Neil's whining caterwaul.

Jameson bobbed his head in approval. "I haven't heard this album in a while."

"No? I was on a big Crue kick for a bit. I hear this band puts on a sick stage show. They were here last August, but we never made it out to see them." The truth was Dad bought us all tickets, but AJ and I didn't think it was appropriate to go without him.

"Yeah, I'd love to see them someday too."

I nodded in agreement. "Me too."

"If they ever come back, cutie, I'm going to take you. I promise." The thought made me grin. The song faded out and another came on, just as raunchy, heavy, and loud as the first. Jameson took a sip of his beer then let the bottleneck dangle from his fingers as he leaned forward on his knees. "You wanna get outta here and go somewhere?"

"Absolutely." I had no idea what he had in mind, and I didn't really care. He could have put me in front of a firing squad, and I would have been happy just being with him in my last hours.

We got into his car, and he backed out of the driveway. He headed toward the center of town and slowed down in front of an old brick building with a green neon sign wearing a gold crown. "Crowne Billiards?" I said, scrunching up my nose.

"You don't play pool?" He looked at me surprised. "C'mon, I'll teach you." He parked around the back and we both got out.

The sound of clanking billiard balls echoed through the dimly lit pool hall. A large man behind the counter looked up from his newspaper as we approached the desk. "What can I do for ya?"

"We'd like a table please, one game," Jameson replied.

The clerk rang us up then set down a triangle shaped rack full of multicolored balls on the counter. "Table twelve in the back." He pointed to the back of the room and the light magically turned on over the pool table. Jameson led the way to the table and placed the triangle on the smooth green felt.

"I'm going to need a stick, right?" I peered around the room trying to figure out where I would acquire such an item.

The look on his face was thoughtful as he considered my question. "You need a stick, huh? You want a big one or a little one?" His brow arched, and I could tell he was holding back a grin when he said it. *Sure, I'll play along.*

My gaze rolled down his body and back up, pausing briefly on the front of his jeans. "A big one." I wanted to sound bold, but my voice came out a lot more timid than I'd hoped. I leaned my hip against the table trying to appear casual.

Coming into my personal space, he looked down at me and licked his lips. "Think you can handle a big stick, little girl?" he whispered in my ear.

The raspy way he whispered, coupled with his breath on my ear, shot my pulse up like a bullet. I crossed one leg over the other trying to smother the sudden arousal burning between them. "Well, there's only one way to find out now, isn't there, big man?" My voice had a slight tremble in it that I hoped he didn't notice. He'd called me a little girl, and I was ready to prove to him that I was anything but. If he'd let me.

He leaned over me at the table and his body pressed against mine for a moment. My pelvis pushed into him with a mind of its own, and his hand steadied my hip. He straightened back to a standing position and whispered again. "Maybe you should acquaint yourself . . ." He grabbed my hand and placed two pool balls into it. " . . . with the balls first."

A silly smirk spread across my face. "Anytime you want me to handle your balls, you just let me know." I turned back toward the table, making sure my ass grazed him in the process. The balls clinked back into their places in the triangle, and I stepped away from him to fetch myself a pool stick. His eyes bored a hole into my back as I went, but I refused to turn around. I sashayed up to the rack, and stood there trying to decide which one I should go with, but I had no idea what I was looking at.

Heavy footsteps came up behind me, but I still refrained from acknowledging them. I felt him at my back, the heat floating off him in waves. He grabbed hold of my hip, his thumb bit into the uncovered area above my jeans, burning my skin and digging hard enough to leave a bruise. "What are you doing, Jillian?" I froze, basking in the warmth of his body and the feel of his skin touching mine.

"What do you mean? I asked, coolly.

"You know what I mean." He grabbed my other hip, squeezing tighter and jerking me against him with both hands. The thick ridge of his arousal pressed against my back, and I hitched in a breath. "It's not a choice you make lightly." His tone was gruff. The complete opposite of his playful demeanor from a few minutes ago.

He dropped his hands and walked closer to the rack,

plucking a stick from it and holding it out for me. "This one looks like it suits you."

I took the stick from his hand. It was small and much less worn than the others on the rack. It looked almost new, like it hadn't been played with since it was placed there. My eyes trailed from the stick back to him. I felt vulnerable under his scrutiny but couldn't tear my eyes from his deep green pools of longing. "Are you sure you're ready?"

"I've never been more ready for anything else in my life." My voice was a whisper. The energy between us was palpable. I gripped the pool stick tight in my hand, watching the way he chewed the inside of his mouth.

"Let's play, then," he said, swiping a stick from the rack and walking back toward the table. My mouth was dry and my insides were shaking. His message came through crystal clear. The electricity we both felt didn't change the fact that he still saw me as an inexperienced little kid. I knew he carried, at least, a candle sized flame for me, but every time I began to feel it burn, he extinguished it from sight. Jameson was never going to make a move. If I wanted something to happen here, it was going to have to be up to me.

Jameson

"NO, I'M STRIPES and you're solids." I laughed. Jillian was a terrible pool player. She obviously had no idea what she was doing, but it was nice watching her try.

"Why am I so bad at this?" she whined.

"You're not bad, you just need practice. Here, let me show you." I saddled up behind her to help her hold the cue better. "Put one hand on the table and make a V with your thumb and pointer finger, like this." I showed her what to do, and she mimicked my position, leaning over the table and putting her little hand next to mine. "Now, slide the stick through the V." I grabbed the cue from behind her and fit it into her hand on the table. "Now, aim." Together, we eyed up the shot and slid the cue back, then quickly tapped the cue ball. It ricocheted off the five ball, sending an orange blur into the corner pocket.

"I did it!" She jumped up and beamed at me.

"You sure did," I said, returning her wide grin. "You'll be hustling games in no time." I leaned over and took a shot of my own. The cue ball missed completely and bounced off all four walls missing every ball on the table. "Dammit, you're rubbing off on me now." She wrinkled up her nose and made a silly face at me.

"Will you help me again?" She stood with the cue next to her, her head cocked to the side. She had an innocent look about her, but I knew what was going on in that beautiful head of hers. I could feel how badly she wanted me, and I hated it. I was a selfish bastard, torturing us both wanting to spend this time with her knowing I couldn't give her what we so desperately wanted.

"You got this. I have faith."

"Please?" She stuck out her bottom lip in a pretty little pout I just couldn't resist. I could handle anything but begging.

"All right, come here." I came up behind her and formed the shot again, only this time she lifted her face and nuzzled my neck. My body tensed up and my insides teemed with conflict from the feeling of her lips on my skin. It felt amazing and wrong at the same time. I wanted to bend her over this table and kiss her senseless, but I also wanted to run from this room for feeling that way. "Jillian?" I meant for it to be a question, but the syllables of her name got caught up in a breath and sounded too excited for my own good.

"You smell delicious," she said, as she caressed my neck with her nose and mouth. Her lips were soft just as I knew they would be. I was dying to drop my face to hers to see how they tasted, but before I had time to act on that impulse, my cell phone buzzed in my pocket. I reached around and dug it out to check the text message that had just come in.

It's getting late. You guys coming back soon?

AJ could add *professional cock block* to his list of accomplishments. "C'mon, Jill, we should get going." I straightened up and she took a step back watching for my reaction to her come on. I racked the balls and carried them back to the counter without looking at her. Jillian just trailed behind me and walked out to the parking lot alone.

I knew my abrupt departure was upsetting to her, but seeing AJ's name pop up on my phone at that exact moment was the buzzkill I needed to fizzle out this intense need I had for her.

We got in the car, and she just stared out the window while we drove back to her house. It killed me that she felt rejected, especially when I wanted her so damn badly, but it was better this way.

I could never be the man she deserved.

When we got back to the house, she couldn't seem to get out of the car fast enough. "Thanks for the pool lesson, Jameson. It was fun." She smiled, but it didn't reach her eyes. I'd hurt her. I should have just said good-bye when we all got back and went the hell home.

"Sure, cutie. I had fun too. Thanks again for the haircut. I'll see you at work tomorrow."

She pressed her lips together with a curt nod before turning her back to me and running toward the house. I idled in the driveway watching her disappear inside, berating myself for being such a jackass.

What the hell was I going to do? If I were smart, I'd just quit the shop and go my own way, but I couldn't do that to AJ. He needed my help there more than I'd initially thought, and I really did need the work. I was stuck between a rock and hard place and had to start thinking about how I was going to get myself out of it without hurting anyone.

CHAPTER NINE

Jillian

IF I COULD crawl into a hole and die right now, I would. I made a bold move, and he'd rejected me. He was laying it on pretty thick, so I thought we were on the same page. How could I have misread his signals so badly?

Am I really so ignorant that I mistook friendly flirting for something more?

Defeated and dejected, I carried myself over to the stairs pausing when AJ called out to me from the family room. He was dressed in sweats, sprawled out on the couch with the remote in his hand and a bag of chips next to him. "You'll ruin your dinner." I curled up on the couch at the opposite end, snatching the bag and pulling out a handful.

"Everything's fine down at the shop," he said fingering the buttons on the remote.

"That's good." I popped a chip in my mouth, letting the salty flavor seep onto my tongue before swallowing it down.

AJ stopped flicking and put the remote down on the armrest next to him. "Did you and Jameson have a good time?" His voice was tight. Like he was forcing himself to be casual but his question had a purpose.

Hearing Jameson's name made my stomach churn. I finished

the handful of chips and rubbed my greasy hands together to get rid of the crumbs, having lost interest in the snack altogether. "Yeah, it was fun. We played pool." It was more than fun. Being with him is like being on a carnival ride. Thrilling and scary at first, but so damn enjoyable that you want to ride it again the second it's over.

That is until you make a move and he walks brusquely away from you, leaving you high and dry.

AJ stared ahead at the TV in front of us, but his eyes weren't focused. He and I had spent so much time together that I could read him like a book. When he's sad, I feel it. Same goes for when he's angry, happy, or any other emotion that rolled past the wall he'd put up around himself. He can't fool me. It all comes through in mannerisms and body language and just plain knowing someone better than they know themselves. He was pussyfooting around the topic, but he had something to say. "What's on your mind, AJ? Just come out with it."

"Just be careful. That's all."

I furrowed my brows together in confusion. "What the hell does that mean?"

"Nothing. Just . . . you don't know him as well as you think you do." He picked up the remote and the incessant flicking started again. This was his way of ending the conversation, but this wasn't over. Not by a long shot.

Heat rolled up my face like a cloud of smoke. Where does every man in my life get off thinking they know what's best for me? I was not a kid anymore. I'd been taking care of myself for a very long time. "And you don't know me as well as *you* think you do, apparently. I don't need your warnings, AJ. You're not my father."

AJ's head snapped in my direction, his jaw set in anger. Bringing up our father was a low blow, and I knew it. AJ had taken it upon himself to fulfill the role as best as he could, and up until now, I'd never thrown it back in his face. My heart still stung from Jameson's dismissal, and AJ was about to get the brunt of it. "For your information, there is nothing going on between Jameson and me, but if there was, I sure as shit wouldn't discuss it with you. Last I checked, I was a grown ass woman. What I do with my body is my own business, not yours, so back the hell off."

AJ's nostrils flared as my harsh words washed over him. We almost never argued, and he seemed surprised by my level of outrage. "I'm not blind. You tell me there's nothing between you, but I call bullshit on that. I see the way he looks at you, Jillian. Like you're an Italian buffet and he wants to fucking eat you. I'm telling you right now the same thing I told him: I'm never going to let it happen. I'll burn the shop to the ground before I see you get tangled up with a guy like him," he growled through his teeth like a rabid wolf.

Suddenly, everything made sense. Jameson's hot and cold behavior, the way he clammed up whenever AJ entered the room. He was warned to stay away from me.

AJ crossed the line this time. I pushed myself off the couch and stood up in front of my brother, glowering at him through narrowed slits. "What gives you the right to tell me who I can and can't be with?" I seethed. "If I wanna fuck Jameson Tate, that's my business, and you do not get a say in it. You don't own me. I'm your sister, not your fucking possession."

I turned on my heel and stormed up to my room, slamming my door shut. Something crashed from downstairs right after. AJ was pissed, but so was I. How dare he involve himself in my affairs? It was completely unacceptable. I'd been on some absurd roller coaster of emotions for weeks, and it was because of AJ all along. Why would Jameson listen to him? Why wouldn't he just tell me my brother was acting like an insane dictator?

The anger had me pacing around my room like a caged animal, wearing a track in the already timeworn hardwood floors. I needed music to drown out the noise in my head. I chose the loudest, raunchiest album I could find, popped it on full volume, and laid on my bed letting it wash over me until I felt calmer. The fan spun lazily overhead, pulling my concentration to the blades instead of thinking about what an incredible butthead my brother was. This bullshit was exhausting. If Jameson wanted me, he'd come to me. Plain and simple.

It was dark out when my eyes popped open. *When did I fall asleep?* The comforter was tangled around my body like an anaconda, and my hair was slicked to the side of my head with sweat. For a second, I didn't even know what day it was, but everything came rushing back as I regained more consciousness. The stereo had been turned off, so AJ must have come in at some point.

My mouth was dry, and I had to pee. I jumped out of bed and headed for the bathroom, passing AJ's room on the way out, but he wasn't inside. It was late. Where was he? I did my business then started down the stairs. The house was dark. AJ wasn't down here either. The light in the fridge was blinding as I tried to grab a water. I winced and looked away, slamming the door shut and welcoming the darkness.

Banging echoed in the distance, and I caught sight of a square of brightness hovering in the pitch black of our backyard.

AJ was playing.

I slid the patio door open to listen better. The cymbals crashed and the snare drum snapped. The steady pounding of the bass drum reverberating in the quiet of night reminded me of a time not too long ago. AJ was upset. He was lashing out on his drum set, burning off whatever aggression he still carried as a result of our fight. I wished I knew what was going on inside that reticent brain of his. He said I didn't know Jameson as well as I thought. Maybe that was true, but what did he know that I didn't?

Jameson

MY STOMACH WAS in knots pulling up to Morello and Son's the next morning. I dreaded seeing her and being forced to look at the hurt I'd put on her face. Just like every morning, she was there, setting up the coffee pot for the day. Her long hair was tied into a messy knot at the nape of her neck. Wispy tendrils fell around her shoulders and ears, and her lips sparkled with fresh pink gloss. She smiled brightly when she saw me coming. Relief washed over me. She wasn't upset anymore. "Hey, you," I said.

"Hey, yourself," she replied smartly. Her eyes danced over me briefly as she made her way back to her desk. My initial assumption was wrong. She was still upset, but there was something more to it than that.

AJ crashed through the back door, scowling at Jillian first, then me, before bursting through the shop door slamming it as he went.

This was bad.

"What was that all about?" I asked her.

"Oh, Stalin and I had a discussion regarding the new sex-free office zone last night." She slapped the spacebar on her keyboard, and the monitor sprang to life. "Seems to be new policy. If he's not gettin' any, neither can anyone else."

I ran my fingers through my hair and scratched my head. "I think you lost me, cutie."

"He told me about the little conversation you guys had. You

know, the one where he gave you a job in lieu of getting in my pants, and you agreed? Well, this is Jillian Morello signing off." She gave me a little salute and turned back toward her monitor. "I'll make it real easy for you to keep that pact."

I was definitely wrong. She was pissed. More than pissed, she was downright hostile.

"Jillian, it's not what you think."

She stared straight ahead at her monitor and answered without missing a beat. "Don't tell me what to think, don't tell me what I need, just go in the shop and do your job." I turned my face to the ceiling and blew out an exasperated breath, then turned and walked out of the office.

AJ was in the process of doing a brake job on a Jeep Cherokee. Now, *I* was mad. It was one thing for him to voice his concerns to me but quite another to tell them to her. "AJ!" I stormed over to him letting the door slam behind me. He glanced at me approach, and then turned back to his work. "What the fuck dude? What did you say to her last night?"

He stopped working on the car long enough to answer the question. "Only what needed to be said. Don't worry, I didn't tell her about your last girlfriend."

I grasped his bicep tightly and jerked him around to face me. "Don't you ever bring that up again," I said evenly. "You don't know shit about what really happened back then. I made you a promise, and I kept it. I never laid a hand on your sister. You fix this thing with Jillian now."

AJ wasn't intimidated in the least, regardless of the height difference between us. He was a tough dude, and I could tell he wasn't going to back down.

"You about done with your rant, Tate? I got work to do." He turned back toward the Jeep the minute I released my grip. I had no idea what happened when I went home yesterday, but today went from bad to worse in lightning speed.

AJ and I worked side by side in silence the rest of the day. Lunchtime came and went, and Jillian never showed her face in the shop once. It was clear this mess wasn't going away as soon as I'd hoped. I felt like ever since I showed up there was nothing but friction. By the end of the day, I was actually exhausted from the tense quiet.

"You want me back tomorrow or what?" I peered at AJ from across the garage waiting for him to tell me to go take a hike.

He lifted his trucker hat by the brim, smoothing his hair back with the opposite hand before replacing it back on his head. "Yeah, man. Come back tomorrow. It's all good." Relieved I still had a job, I flicked my chin in his direction and walked out the bay doors.

Jillian was waiting for me in the parking lot. The gentle wind picked up the loose strands of hair and blew them around her face. She leaned against my license plate, elbows resting on the trunk as the sun behind her created an angelic effect around her body. "You lost?" I said.

She cocked her head as I approached, the tiny diamond stud in her nose catching the light just right. "I think we need to talk," she said, crossing her arms over her ample chest pushing her tits up to the neckline of her shirt. I wondered if she did it on purpose just to screw with me.

"What about?" A piece of hair blew across her mouth and stuck to her lips. I reached out and rescued it from its lip-gloss prison, sticking it behind her ear, but she recoiled at my touch like it burned her.

"About this, Jameson." She rubbed her cheek on her shoulder, wiping me off her. "If you and I can't . . . If we can't be together, you need to stop all this." The look of desperation in her eyes was hard to face.

"Stop all what, Jillian?" I linked my thumbs into the pockets of my jeans to keep from touching her again as I waited for her to explain.

Her arms dropped to her sides in huff. She pursed her lips and her eyes fell to the ground before starting again. "Are we friends, Jameson?"

"Of course, we're friends, cutie. You know that." I lowered my head slightly to try to catch her eyes with mine. She found my gaze, locking on it and blinking her long lashes at me.

"AJ is your friend too, right?"

I raised an eyebrow unsure of where she was going with this. "Yeah, sure."

"Do you hug AJ? Run your fingers through his hair? Hold his hand, make dirty innuendos . . . all those little things you do with me?" Her voice was thick, sorrowful. She pinned me in place with her dark gaze and waited for me to answer.

A lump formed in my throat, and I swallowed hard. I finally understood what it was she was trying to say. "No, Jillian. I don't."

She took a deep breath, and her eyes began to sparkle in the late day sun. She was holding it back, but she wanted to cry. "Then this needs to stop. You need to treat me like you would AJ. Like you would any other friend. You're just . . . not being fair." A tear rolled down her cheek then another. I wanted so desperately to wipe them away. To hold her and kiss her until those gorgeous lips were swollen, but that was the exact opposite of what she needed from me. She was asking me to leave her alone. She was accepting our situation and trying to make it right.

I stayed there with my hands in my pockets, unsure of what I could possibly say to the beautiful heartbroken girl in front of me. She wiped her face and straightened her shoulders. "That's all I need to say." Then she walked away and disappeared behind the building, leaving me standing there freezing in the hot July sun.

CHAPTER TEN

Jillian

I WALKED INTO the house feeling hollow, afraid that if I moved too fast, the shattered remains of my heart would rattle around in my chest and cut my other organs. My anger from this morning dissipated somewhere around lunchtime, and I knew what I had to do to fix it and make everyone happy. I gave him the out he was looking for, the one AJ expected, and the one that left a little piece of my soul clinging to that Mustang in the parking lot.

We were never really together, but knowing we never will be was more painful than I expected. My chest ached with the resolve that I would only ever be his friend. That I might some-day have to live through seeing him with another girl, one who he felt would suit him better.

I moved around the kitchen like a zombie preparing dinner for AJ's arrival home. I never brought him lunch today, and I knew he would be starving. This was my peace offering. *He'll forget and I'll forgive, and we'll continue our lives like we always have.* It was just the way it went.

With the timer on the oven set, I retreated to my room. It had barely changed since I was a girl, and I suddenly hated everything about it. My mom handed down the old French provincial-style furniture from when she was a kid. The gold paint on the edges was all worn away and the bottoms of the drawers had since been replaced due to decay. I'd lined the walls with various posters when I was an early teen, rebelling against the childish room I'd been saddled with, and they remained there to this day. The only real change was the blankets on the full-size bed. Once white with yellow daisies, I'd replaced the comforter for one that was a simple black and gray. The room was a mishmash of things I've collected throughout the years, showcasing the many changes I'd been through in the years I've lived there. It was an odd contrast between youth and adult, an exact parallel to me. While I was a woman in many ways, I was still a child in so many others.

The front door opened and closed downstairs, and AJ's heavy boots hit the floor on the mat in the foyer. The stairs creaked under his weight as he ascended, most likely seeking out a shower like every day. "Jill?" I rolled over on my bed and saw him filling up my doorway. He was still in his coveralls and a black mark was on his forehead from where he probably touched it after changing someone's oil. "You all right?"

Sitting up to greet my brother, I pulled my knees to my chest. He looked tired, and I wondered what time he'd come in from the garage last night. "Yeah, AJ, I'm fine. Just sleepy. It's been a long day. Dinner's in the oven."

"Okay. Just making sure." He stayed leaned against my doorway, his eyes flitting around the room.

"Is there something else?"

His gaze landed on me at my question. He was reading my face, trying to gauge whether or not I was still angry with him. "No, just checking in. I'm going to take a shower. I'll see you downstairs." He backed up and walked away, and I heard the shower start up down the hall. I rubbed my face and jumped off my bed, resigning myself to move past all of it.

⁓

THE OLD ADAGE was true. Be careful what you wished for, you just might get it. I told him to leave me alone, and he listened. I barely saw Jameson all week. He waited in his car until AJ was here then headed straight for the bay doors instead of coming in through the office as usual. I missed our morning routine, but it was for the best.

Saturday morning, I dragged myself into the office. Saturdays were our busiest day, and I was looking forward to a lazy Sunday. I pulled the keyboard tray out to start my work and found an envelope with my name scrawled across the front. The tiny cursive letters looked meticulously written, almost like a font on the computer. It wasn't AJ's chicken scratch handwriting. I tore open the flap and pulled out the flier inside.

Free Concert in the Park! Wild Side,
NJ's Premier Motley Crue Tribute Band.
Saturday, July 11.

I turned the flier over and the same excellent cursive was on the back.

I know it's not the real Crue, but it should be fun nonetheless.
Surely, it's OK for two friends to hang out sometimes.

A smile crept across my face betraying the warning in my head that this was a bad idea. My heart pounded in my chest. It was the first time I'd felt anything since our conversation last Monday morning.

I was still smiling like a buffoon when AJ came in the back door. He stopped at the percolator to pour himself a cup of coffee before starting his day. "What's gotten you so happy?" he asked, noticing my unusually bright mood.

I folded up the flier and stuck it back in the envelope where it came from. "Just had a good night's sleep, I guess." I got up to pour myself a cup of coffee alongside him. "What's the plan for tonight?" I asked casually, testing him to see if he already knew about the concert in the park.

He shook his head as he blew on the boiling hot cup of black liquid before taking a tiny sip. He winced as it touched his tongue, and he blew on it a second time. "Nothing fun. Just planning on hanging out at home. Why, what's up?"

I dumped some cream into my cup and stirred more then I needed to, just to avoid looking at him as I prepared to lie to his face. "Oh, nothing. Thinking about getting together with a friend later. Just making sure it's cool if I used the truck."

Among the many other things we shared ownership of, one was our dad's truck. It was a beat-up old green Chevy pickup with well over a hundred thousand miles on it, but it was still kicking and got us where we needed to go. I was frequently the only one who drove it. AJ had his own car, a blue '85 Firebird, but I still felt the need to ask every time I took it out just in case. AJ's car was a pile of crap that he repaired more often than he drove.

"Yeah, sis, have at it. You should get together with your friends more. Who you seeing tonight? Stephanie or Megan?" AJ asked, cupping imaginary breasts in front of him when he said Megan's name. Spoiler alert, her boobs weren't even real.

I shrugged and turned back toward my desk. "Maybe both." My palms were clammy as I pushed papers around my desk, trying to look busy so he'd go away and not ask any more questions. I never was the best at lying, especially to AJ. When we were kids, he usually was the one who lied for the both of us while I hid behind him, my facial expression giving us away. I should just be a grownup and tell him that Jameson and I were going out together, but I didn't want to deal with another confrontation. It was just easier not to mention it. After all, it was innocent, right?

Jameson's car rumbled into the lot as AJ snapped the lid onto his coffee and walked out into the shop. He parked and got out, walking through the bay doors just as he had all week, but this time, he looked in the direction of the office. We locked eyes through the window. I put my finger to my lips hoping he understood my message. AJ wasn't to know we had plans. He winked and turned away, his poker face flawless, walking farther into the shop to start his work for the day.

Jameson

I TRIED TO stay away from her. I really did. It was five of the longest days of my life. When I saw the flier for the concert in the park, my heart swelled knowing how much Jill would enjoy it. It was a sign. We were meant to be friends. We could do this.

AJ made a quick run to the auto parts store, and I took that opportunity to talk to her. Jillian was sitting at her desk with a pile of receipts in front of her. She heard me approach and looked up from her work. "Hey, Jame, long time no see." Her voice was like magic. Hearing it after five days was like seeing the ocean for the first time. It relaxed and excited me instantly.

I leaned over the desk so I could see her better. God, she was beautiful. The word friends flashed in the forefront of my mind, and I settled down on the couch instead. "So you in for Wild Side tonight?"

Her smile brightened, and she held up the envelope I'd left for her. "Yeah, I'm in." She licked her lips and her smile faded a bit. "Listen, would it be cool if we didn't mention this to AJ? It's just . . . he worries, you know? I don't want to upset him."

"Yeah, sure, that's fine. I mean there isn't really much to say.

Two friends hanging out, right?" I was trying to sound sincere, but hearing it come out of my mouth, I was unconvinced. As painful as it was, I pushed our talk from Monday into my mind. I forced myself to remember the anguish on her face to keep from acting foolish and messing this up. I only had one chance to do this, and I had to do it right.

"So I guess I'll just meet you there. Sound good?" She looked at me for approval, her big brown eyes breaking down my resolve.

"Sounds great," I said rising to my feet and returning to the shop.

Later that night, I was sitting in my car at the park waiting for her to arrive. Having hung out with Jill constantly over the past month, I couldn't figure out why my stomach was twisted up the way it was. A Chevy S-10 pulled into the lot and parked next to me and all my innards jumped for joy. *She was here.*

The door to the truck opened, and she stepped out. My heart pounded in my chest, and I swore I was either having a heart attack or the best damn dream of my life. She was wearing a dress. It was all black with a purple skull and crossbones on the chest. It came down low in the front and clung to her torso like a second skin, then fanned out around her hips. Her normally clear lips were stained ruby red and black eyeliner ringed her eyes.

I was completely fucked.

"Hey there, *friend*." I wanted to compliment her and tell her how gorgeous she looked, but I warned myself against it. After all, I wouldn't tell AJ he was hot, right?

I stuck out my hand to give her a handshake. She giggled and slipped hers inside. "Nice to see you too, *friend*."

We walked up to the park together and laid a blanket on the ground before settling in. She leaned back on her palms, legs stretched out in front of her, crossed at the ankles, sandals laid forgotten on the blanket next to her feet. I made it a point to sit on the other side and put the cooler I'd brought between us as a barrier to keep me from touching her pale skin. I'd packed us a couple of soda bottles spiked with rum in case she wanted to drink, and a few waters in case she didn't.

For a tribute band, Wild Side was surprisingly good. The lead singer couldn't exactly hit all the notes Vince Neil could, but the band was spot on. We joked about the way they had on the same platform heels and makeup the real band wore, and wondered where the hell they bought that shit in the first place.

"Do you think the bass player is going to set himself on fire?" She sat up straighter pulling her legs under her, craning her neck so she could see better. Her excitement at seeing this small local band was infectious. Jillian didn't get happy like a normal person. She radiated it. You could almost feel it emanating off her body.

She reached into the cooler to get a soda. The whole damn thing fell over slinging shards of ice all over the blanket. "Shit, that was graceful," she cursed.

After I had helped her scoop the ice back in, she pushed the cooler to the back of the blanket to cover the wet spot, leaving the area between us exposed. Without that barrier, she sat closer than she was before. Too close. Her fruity perfume invaded my nostrils making it hard to concentrate on anything else. She smelled so fucking good I could almost taste it.

I kept side eyeing her, watching without wanting her to know I was a total creeper. Her head tipped back as the soda bottle touched her lips. I watched the graceful way her throat moved as she swallowed. A rogue drop broke free, rolling down her chin, cascading past her neck, and disappearing between her breasts.

My eyes closed in a valiant attempt to remove the mental image and keep my dick from bursting out of my pants. My body didn't exactly have the same plans of friendship that my head did. I mentally counted to ten and opened them. She had settled back on the blanket resting on her hands and watching the band.

The lights from the stage twinkled in her eyes, and her chocolate hair blew in the warm summer breeze. She looked like an angel in the darkness. I knew it was wrong. I promised that we would just be friends, and I meant it. But seeing her, stretched out on the ground, her face just inches from mine, I couldn't hold it back anymore.

She licked her lips, playing with her gloss as she always did, and brushed her hair back off her shoulder. That simple movement drew me in. I hooked my arm around her back, pulling her against me and pressed my lips to hers. She gasped against my mouth, my unexpected advance catching her off guard. Fire alarms went off in my mind warning me to get the hell out of there, but once I'd started, there was no way I was stopping.

Cherry. That was the taste I'd been dying for since the day I walked into the shop over a month ago. The sticky flavoring gracing her luscious lips that kept me awake at night was no longer a mystery. They moved against mine, slow and tentative, her tongue grazing along the edge of my lips, begging for entry into my mouth.

A soft growl rumbled in my chest. I pulled her bottom lip into my mouth devouring her cherry flavored gloss and letting it slide through my teeth before trailing down her neck. "Jameson," she breathed. "We should go."

We separated, chests heaving with panting breaths. She sat on the blanket and stared up through her thick black lashes, her crimson gloss smeared around her puffy lips. The band was still playing in the background, but it was long forgotten by both of us. Our hands clasped together, and I pulled her to her feet then collected our things to walk back to the car.

I'd broken my promise to her and to AJ. It was foolish to think I could keep our relationship on a friendly level. I'd crossed a line, and there was no turning back. Jillian Morello was a drug, and I was completely addicted to her.

CHAPTER ELEVEN

Jillian

HE KISSED ME. His lips were skilled and strong just like the rest of him was. It was unexpected and intimidating, and I wanted it more than I'd wanted anything else in my entire life.

As we walked back to the parking lot, I felt like I was floating. My body was filled with helium and he was pulling me to his car by a string. If he were to let go, I'd probably fly into the atmosphere and never return. I leaned against the door in a daze, as if I was drunk on him, as he packed his things back in the trunk.

His body language was stiff as he came to face me. He looked guilty, like the cat who ate the canary. "Jillian, I . . ." I didn't want to hear what he had to say next, worried he thought it was a mistake. I wrapped my fist in his shirt and pulled him close to me. Once he was within reach, my other hand found the nape of his neck, pulling his head in to fuse our lips together a second time. He didn't hold back. He pinned me between him and the car, and I wanted to breathe him in until he was a part of me.

Every part of my body felt awake. It tingled from my head down to my toes, and I never wanted it to end. His hands were lost in my hair as our tongues twirled together. The band wailed in the background and people floated around us, but I didn't care. The only thing that mattered at this exact moment was how delectable his mouth tasted, and how incredible his body felt pressed against mine.

My hands slid down his strong back and inched up his shirt, tracing the hard lines of muscle along his stomach with my fingertips. He groaned but pulled away, taking a quick step back. "We have to stop." His breathing was heavy, and his voice was thick.

"Why?" I never wanted him to stop. I wanted him to cover me in his delectable kisses from head to toe and send me into oblivion. I wanted to see if the rest of him was as strong and pleasurable as his mouth was.

"Because if it goes any further, I won't be able to." His hand ran through my hair and down my neck. "Because I want to kiss you here . . ." he placed a kiss on my jaw " . . . and here . . ." another under my ear " . . . and here . . ." and another on my collar bone " . . . and so many other places we just don't have time for tonight."

"No one's watching the clock, Jameson," I said in a strained voice, my body still trembling from the feeling of his lips.

His mouth curled into a heavenly little smile. "It's a marathon, cutie, not a sprint. I promise you it will be worth the wait." He lowered his lips to mine again, a soft end of date kiss that was as sweet as the soda that lingered on his tongue.

"Get home safe," he said, helping me into the truck and closing the door.

I drove home in a fog of lust blanketed in disappointment. He promised it would be worth the wait, but I'd waited so long already. Pulling into the driveway, I still felt him all around me. The smell of him on my skin and the taste of him on my lips served as a prequel of what I hoped was to come. I opened the front door quietly, hoping AJ was already asleep, but wasn't that lucky. He was on the couch in sweatpants and a tee shirt. A row of empty bottles were clustered together on the end table where our lamp used to be until he broke it in a fit of rage. "Hey, sis, how was your night?"

I wanted to run straight up the stairs, but his voice stopped me in the foyer. "Oh, you know, coffee and gossip. Normal stuff." I subconsciously touched my fingers to my lips as another lie tumbled out of my mouth.

"Spending time with girls is good for you. One night and you're already starting to look like one." He tipped his bottle in my direction gesturing to my dress before taking a sip.

I rolled my eyes and put my hand on my hip. "Ha, ha, I didn't realize you were a comedian," I said flatly. He responded with a snort. It was obvious he'd had a few already.

"How many beers have you had tonight, dude?"

"I don't know. Enough, I guess." He drained the bottle, and dropped it on the side table next to the others with a clink. It was normal for him to drink a beer or two after work, but kind of unusual for him to get carried away. AJ rarely, if ever, allowed himself to lose control.

"Well, I'm going up to bed. Good night." I turned and ran up the stairs thankful to have gotten away with my story for the night.

It was hot as Hades in there. I stripped off my dress and crawled into bed in my bra and panties. Conflicted feelings attacked my subconscious. I hated lying to AJ, but after what happened between Jameson and me, I was happy I hadn't told him we were together. If this was going to continue, we were going to have to be extra careful.

Thoughts of Jameson occupied my mind, and I wondered what he was doing at that moment. Whether he was lying down thinking about me, and if he was as wound up as I was. I imagined him naked in his bed, his rock hard body quivering as he satisfied his agonizing need for me.

My eyes closed and my hand moved down inside my panties to soothe my own ache. It moved skillfully, as I tried to imagine it was his hand on my body and his kisses still burning on my skin. I thought back to how deftly his fingers moved along the frets of his guitar as my own fingers explored the untouched regions of my anatomy. The fantasy of him pushing himself into me, filling me completely and squelching this need I lived with day in and day out pushed me gratefully to orgasm. I pinched my eyes shut and bit down on my lip to stifle any noise, hoping not to be heard as his name escaped my lips. Finally able to relax, I drifted off to sleep with memories of Jameson on my mind.

It was early when I woke up the next morning. My room was blazing hot, and I couldn't tell if it was the temperature outside or my dreams causing the sheen of sweat dappling my bare skin. I kicked off the blankets and pushed myself off the bed, rustling around a clean laundry basket for a shirt and shorts to throw on before going downstairs.

AJ was asleep on the couch, and the television still glowed in front of him. I felt guilty seeing him there. My brother was my best friend and my protector, and I lied straight to his face yesterday. Why did it have to be so difficult? I would love nothing more than to shake him awake and tell him everything. To come clean and admit that yes I had feelings for Jameson, and no I refused to set them aside because he was jealous that I was messing around with his friend. But I just couldn't do that. AJ had made his opinions known, and that was the end of it.

Jameson

I TOSSED AND turned most of that night thinking about what an impulsive idiot I was. *I should regret kissing her, but I don't.*

Not one bit. Sure, it complicated things around the shop, but I couldn't deny her anymore. Her fruity perfume lingered on my skin when I got out of bed in the morning, and it made me almost dizzy. She felt amazing in my arms. What the hell was I gonna do?

Her soft, supple lips were still on my mind when my phone started to ring. My boner deflated instantly when I saw it was AJ. *Fuck.* I gave the screen a quick swipe and braced myself for the possibility of a shit storm. "Hey man, what's up?"

"Hey, bro. You're coming in tomorrow, right? The schedule is pretty packed."

"Yeah sure, I'll be in if you need me to be."

"Cool. Oh, and one more thing. I was a dick last week, man. I don't know what the fuck got into me. We cool?" Hearing AJ apologize to me after last night made me cringe.

"Uh, yeah man, we're cool. Don't worry about it." I disconnected the call and pushed my hair back with my hands. He didn't know about last night. We were safe for now. But how would the scenario Monday play out? Holding back from grabbing Jill and making her mine was going to be hard as hell, especially now that I've crossed that line. I finally knew first hand that her skin tasted as sweet as it smelled, and now, I was starving for it.

Monday morning couldn't come fast enough. I'd never been so excited to go to work in my life. Unable to sleep, I ended up getting there early. I watched her come toward me. The tinkling sound of metal on metal carried through the wind from the keys that dangled from her petite finger. A dazzling smile split her face when she saw me waiting for her. "Hey, friend," I said.

"You're early today. Kissing up to the boss?" she asked stopping in front of me.

My finger hooked through the belt loop of her jeans and

pulled her to me. "Nah, just kissing her." I dipped my head and planted my mouth onto her cherry lips. Her body sagged into mine, and I held her close, cupping her round ass in my hand.

"Good morning to you too." She sighed.

"It is now," I replied, gently taking hold of her wrist as she swiped her thumb across my mouth to wipe away the residual gloss. The smell of citrus rose off her skin. I skimmed my nose across her wrist, pressing my lips against her beating pulse.

"We should go in." She continued her walk toward the entrance pulling me along with her hand in hand. Once inside, she went about her business. The computer hummed to life and the smell of coffee rivaled the stagnant odor of lingering grease as she began scooping grinds into the percolator. My arms encircled her from behind. The way she melted against me every time I touched her sent a testosterone-fueled shot of possessiveness rocketing through my veins.

I took her earlobe between my teeth, tonguing the row of tiny hoops that traveled halfway up. She moaned, and I tightened my grip, splaying my hand across her stomach and feeling the entire length of her pressed against me. "AJ will be here any minute." Her breathy voice did little to squash the budding arousal that was growing by the second. She was right, though. Getting caught by AJ would not be good.

Stepping back, I leaned my ass against her desk and shoved my hands into my pockets. "How are we going to do this, cutie? It's not even nine a.m., and I'm already having trouble keeping my hands off you."

She finished preparing the coffee and turned to face me with a shrug. The back door opened at that exact moment, and AJ came in. "Mornin'"

"Morning, AJ. Coffee's brewing." Jillian didn't look over at me again as she plopped down at her desk to get to work. AJ walked into the shop, and I obediently followed.

AJ wasn't kidding when he said the schedule was busy. I didn't look up from my work until Jillian came out to tell us she was heading home for lunch. "I'll bring you something back, okay, AJ?"

He grumbled a reply and her glare fell on me. "What about you, Jameson? Anything special you want?" The question seemed so innocent, but it was laced with hidden meaning and I read it loud and clear.

"Actually, I got some shit I gotta get done. Mind if I take the hour, AJ?" I didn't look at Jillian as I said it.

Jillian's gaze grazed past me as she walked out of the shop. "I'll see you boys in an hour."

AJ wiped his hands on a rag and threw it to the side. "Yeah, man, go ahead. I'll hold down the fort here."

I stopped in the bathroom and washed up before heading out to lunch. My stomach twisted as I got in my car and drove around the block. A liquor store sat beyond a row of trees behind their house. I parked in the lot and bolted back through the shallow woods. She was waiting at the back door for me. I ran through the yard and didn't stop until my lips descended onto hers. "I knew you'd come," she said, backing into the dining room on her tiptoes, tugging me by the shirt.

Jillian's ass hit the table pushing it across the hardwood floor with a screech. I lifted her up and dropped her on the edge, closing the vast height difference between us. The burning heat between her legs caught me off guard as she squeezed them around me. She was so turned on by one little kiss. Sinking myself into that molten pit of fire now would incinerate my dick to soot, but still it pressed against my fly begging for the chance to find out.

Her fingernails scratched at my skin, clawing at the hem of my shirt and pulling it over my back. "Your shirt is filthy, take it off," she demanded between kisses. We separated long enough to rip the grease-stained tee over my head then crashed back together.

My lips attacked her neck as I tugged at the knot in the back of her T-shirt. It held tight. That stupid tie must have been an indestructible force in the universe. The only thing that stood between me and probably the greatest set of tits I'd ever witness in my life was a thin sheet of cotton held tight by a fucking knot that I couldn't budge if my life depended on it.

"Having trouble, Tate?" She laughed as she sensed my growing frustration. Behind her back, she swiftly yanked the knot free and the oversized shirt billowed out, hiding her figure from sight. She pushed me back to lift the shirt over her head and dropped it on the table next to her.

Jackpot.

The simple black bra was nothing fancy, but my God all the blood drained from my body instantly. The round swells of her breasts rose out of the shiny black fabric like two smooth mountains of awesomeness. Her skin was like silk against my hands. Her head fell back, inviting my lips to the places previously covered by her shirt.

"Jesus, every fucking inch of you smells like candy." The tip of my tongue traced the valley between her tits. She fell back on her hands, and I kissed a trail down her stomach sweeping my tongue over her belly button. "Mmm, it tastes like it too," I groaned.

A trail of saliva shimmered along her skin as I licked my way back up and captured her mouth again. Her soft chest pressed against mine, the skin-on-skin contact driving me crazy with want. The urge to rip the rest of her clothes off and have my way with her in the very spot she and AJ share their meals slowly overtook me, but I resisted. We only had an hour together, and I didn't want to start something we didn't have time to finish. When I eventually made her mine, it was going to be epic.

Somewhere in the distance, church bells chimed once. Our time together was up, but she squeezed her legs tighter around me making it incredibly hard to break away. "Jillian," I said on her lips. "I have to get back."

One hour just wasn't enough time. I was nowhere near done with my exploration of her body, but duty called and I had to go. "But you haven't even eaten yet," she said, looking as disappointed as I felt. Believe it or not, that question *was* innocent.

I dragged my mind up from the gutter with a smirk. Her concern for my wellbeing was sweet. "It's fine, cutie. I'll live." My lips found hers again before picking up my shirt to go back to work.

Jill rested on her hand, her lips swollen and her skin flushed with arousal. "I could open the office early tomorrow. If you want."

"Definitely," I said and jogged back to my car.

CHAPTER TWELVE

Jillian

HOW THE HELL was I expected to go back to work after that? My entire body felt like it was about to burst into flames. *A cold shower, ice cream, snow . . .* My mind flipped through a catalog of frozen things trying to extinguish the burning inside me as I ran around the kitchen making AJ a sandwich.

Settling back at my desk to finish out the day, a folded slip of paper stuck out from under my phone and caught my eye. The tiny cursive letters inside made my heart race instantly.

To be continued, 8 a.m. tomorrow

I couldn't help the smile that crept onto my face. Every place his lips touched was practically thrumming with delight. I finished the afternoon in a blur, unable to think about anything besides Jameson's lips and hands, getting very little accomplished.

By seven the next morning, I was awake, dressed, and watching the clock. As hilarious as it was watching him struggle with my tee shirt, I opted to just leave it long for now. I wondered how long it was going to last. Would Jameson get tired of all this sneaking around and move on? Was I prepared to deal with that when it eventually happened?

I felt like there was a possibility that I'd wanted him from the moment I saw him. Not just this last month, but years ago when we first met as kids in my garage. I had a silly little crush on him then, but it was just kid stuff. He'd make a joke, and I'd giggle like a fool. I was stupid and immature, self-conscious and unsure of my own feelings. Maybe he was the reason I never even considered being with anyone else. Jameson took my world by storm the moment I laid eyes on him all those years ago.

It took his return for me to realize that Jameson Tate had been in the back of my mind all this time.

Five years he was gone. Had he not returned, I might never have met another man who made me feel the way he does. The thought of him leaving again terrified me. Even worse than that, the idea that he'd eventually get bored with me tore me open and left me feeling gutted.

The Budweiser clock on the office wall said seven fifty-five. Jameson would be here any minute. Anxious and nervous, I sat on the couch and waited. My knee bounced to the beat of my heart, and I had to cross my legs to stop it. I twirled my hair so many times that morning with anticipation that I was about to become bald, my inexperience making me feel vulnerable.

What if I didn't know how to please him?

As usual, I heard him coming before he came into sight. The roar of the engine excited me, and I sat up straighter, aroused and eager to see him. He walked through the door and smiled, his lopsided grin easing my anxiety. The morning light sliced through the door and lit his green eyes up like brilliant gemstones. His face was freshly shaven and his damp hair was combed back out of his eyes. My already racing heart thundered in my chest. I stood to greet him at the door. "Hey, friend," I said, reiterating his greeting from the previous morning.

"Oh, I think we're way past that, cutie." He grinned wickedly and wrapped his arms around me. My face was even with his chest and I squeezed him to me, inhaling his clean scent before sitting back down on the worn leather sofa.

With both arms resting along the back of the couch, I crossed my legs in my best attempt at a Sharon Stone impersonation. "So you have me here now. What ever will you do with me?" I said, batting my eyelashes with a dramatic flair of innocence.

The way he licked his lips and peered down at me caused a small family of butterflies to flutter around in my stomach. "Oh, I'm sure I can think of a few things." He lowered himself onto his knees in front of me and dropped his mouth to mine. I parted my lips, granting his minty tongue entry. "That was certainly a good start."

"Come up here with me." I tugged at his body pulling him onto the couch next to me. "That's better." Our lips met again, and he lowered my back to the rich warm leather. His large body covered my smaller one. Those bothersome butterflies flapped around in my gut, whirling and churning things deep within. I was in over my head. Hardness poked through his jeans, a thick rigid bulge that ground into me as his hands hooked under my knees and wrapped my legs around him.

Lust flowed through me like a river of lava threatening to burn me to ash. His taste, his smell, and that delicious thing he did with his tongue caused my pelvis to move with a mind of its own. His hand slithered between our bodies cupping my mound and teasing me through the thick fabric of my jeans. "Jesus Jill, you're on fire," he said, undoing my pants and slipping his hand inside.

The feeling of his calloused fingers on my bare flesh was new and thrilling. My hips bucked into his hand, but he pulled it out too soon, sitting up and sliding my arousal between the tips of his middle finger and thumb.

The look on his face was downright villainous. He tugged at my jeans, vigorously pulling both them and my underwear down my legs at the same time, dropping them on the dirty tile. A rush of cool air blew across my hot center as he pushed my knees apart, his eyes darkening as he looked at my naked bottom half.

AJ's words fluttered into my mind. *You're an Italian buffet, and he wants to eat you.* Nerves gripped hold of my body as he kissed my calf and trailed his way down, stopping to nip at my thigh. His tongue flicked the sensitive flesh between my legs and I sucked in a breath, scooting backward from the shocking sensation. "Relax, cutie, I'll take care of you."

Unable to form actual sentences, I nodded. He gripped my hips and pulled me toward him with a gentle force that assured me he was a man of his word. He tasted me again, softer this time, slow and languid. I breathed out a long, slow breath, and my head fell to the side

He dipped between my folds, and I whimpered. My hand shot to my mouth, embarrassed over my own breathy noise. His licks got more intense, harder and rougher. He exhaled a hot breath teasing the nub with the tip of his tongue causing me to bite down hard on my bottom lip.

Splayed out like this, the couch was too small for us both to fit. He slumped off the side, bringing one of my legs with him over his shoulder, the other remaining bent at the knee, foot flat on the cushion.

Stretched to capacity, he tongue fucked me mercilessly. Pressure erupted down below as his thick finger slid inside me knuckle deep. A loud moan catapulted out of my mouth. I bit down on the throw pillow some old customer made with our family's name on it to drown out the unavoidable sounds vibrating out of my chest. My fingernails bit into the arms of the couch above my head, making crescent shaped divots in the old beat up leather. His tongue continued its heavenly whirl around my throbbing clit, and my hips moved with the same delectable rhythm of it. A rhythm that was so fucking spot on, I was seconds from spontaneously combusting from the sheer pleasure of it. "That's it, Jill. Let it go."

Jameson's finger stroked me from the inside, scraping the calloused tip along my inner walls with precise accuracy. The soundtrack was a duet of heavy breathing, squeaks, and squeals as his mouth slurped and groaned. I felt like he was eating me alive. I was so close it was agonizing.

He sucked hard, and my back vaulted off the couch violently as I came. Holy shit, I came hard. Pops of light flashed behind my eyelids, and a vulgar stream of expletives ripped from the back of my throat. His fingers dug into my hips to keep me from flying off the couch. He licked me gently as I floated back down from the most intense experience of my life.

"Fuck, you're delicious." My lashes fluttered open and locked on a set of emeralds shining with carnivorous greed. He sucked his finger into his mouth, the one covered in me, and licked his lips. "I want to eat you for breakfast every morning," he mumbled.

Panting like a dog, I laid on the couch unable to move. I felt dizzy and brainless. My limbs were Jell-O and I swear to Christ my toes were numb. Jameson slid my underwear on first while I was still lying down, and then pulled me to a standing position so I could get my jeans on. His face wore a triumphant grin as I stumbled on shaky legs like a baby deer, trying to pull up pants that were probably too tight to begin with, a side effect from having to shop from the children's rack. I slid my sneakers back on, thankful that I never actually tied the laces as AJ came in through the back door. I opened my mouth to say hello but all that came out was a squeaky noise.

"What's with you?" he asked, looking at me puzzled.

"Huh?" I said stupidly.

"You're white as a ghost. You all right?"

I was still reeling from the sensation of Jameson's head between my thighs and couldn't get my brain to function. "Oh, Jillian saw a spider. Big sucker. Scared the shit out of her." The lie seemed to tumble out of Jameson's mouth so easily. His calm exterior was surprising for someone whose face was buried in my goodies just five minutes ago.

"Girls," AJ snorted. "I bet you rescued the damn thing like a pussy too, instead of just squashing it." Embarrassment actually flashed on Jameson's face.

"Whatever, dude," he said flipping AJ the bird before turning his attention back to me. "If you need anything else, Miss Morello, you just let me know." From the corner of my eye, I saw him suck his lips into his mouth again as he went back toward the shop and a chill spread through me.

"He rescues bugs?" I asked AJ, starting to regain the feeling in my lower extremities.

"He always used to. I killed a moth once and he freaked out. He's an interesting fellow indeed." My heart melted. I hated bugs, but the fact that a big, strong guy like him took the time to save them was probably the cutest thing I'd ever heard.

AJ started cluelessly tinkering with the percolator. *Amazing, this guy can rebuild a transmission with his bare hands, but he can't seem to figure out how to brew a simple cup of coffee.*

"I got it, go work." I gave him a playful little push and set out to start my day.

Jameson

JILLIAN AND I met every morning that week. Sometimes, we messed around on the couch, and other times, we just sat together and shot the shit. My favorite were the times we did both.

I loved talking to her. She was funny and cute and had the best laugh I'd ever heard in my life. It had started to become routine, one I looked forward to all day long. She was a better wakeup call than any cup of coffee. The only thing better would be waking up with her in my bed. Someday, I told myself, I'd have the kind of place I could bring her to. One where we could be alone. Preferably not one where I shared a communal bathroom with a bunch of dirty vagrants. I was still working on that one.

When I pulled into the office that rainy Saturday, she was waiting for me as she'd been all week. Her hair was damp from her run to the shop, and I thought back to Fourth of July weekend when she walked out of the bathroom in her towel.

I flopped onto the couch bringing her down on my lap, her petite frame tucked under my arm. My fingers burrowed through the dark curtain of her hair and ran up and down the creamy smoothness of her neck. It was so natural, sitting on the couch wrapped in each other's embrace as if we belonged together. "I love how soft your skin is." She sighed and snuggled in closer. "And I love the way your body fits against mine."

She sat up and kicked her leg out, straddling me face to face. "What else?" she asked with a playful grin.

Our lips met in a soft kiss. "I love how sweet your lips are." My mouth pressed against her collarbone next and I swiped my nose back and forth against it like an Eskimo. "And how delicious you always smell," I continued, slipping my hands down the length of her. "And definitely how sexy your body is." My fingertip ran between her legs, and she giggled. "How burning hot you always are." It slid up her stomach and between her breasts, stopping in the center of her chest. "But I love this the most."

"What's that?" she asked with a slight tilt of her head.

"Your heart." I pulled her in and placed a kiss over it.

"My heart?" she said with an arched brow, surprised by my answer.

"Yep. Of course, I appreciate the pretty wrapping, but I also know the real gift is what's inside." I rested my palm over her heart. Its rapid-fire beating matched my own. "Every morning, I see you waiting here for me, and I feel honored. Not only because you let me tear open the beautiful paper but also because I'm able to get a glimpse of the unique gift that is you."

I laid a hand on her face and her deep brown eyes filled with warmth. She kissed me again, and I wrapped my arms around her back as we lowered to the couch. Her legs lifted around my waist. It was instinct at this point. We were running out of time to do anything else, but I was more than happy to stay there for as long as I was able to.

IT WAS LATE in the afternoon when Jillian poked her head out of the office door into the shop. "AJ! Phone!" She ran out the door and hopped around on the balls of her feet, stopping in front of AJ. "Some guy wants to discuss a restoration with you. '57 Corvette," she said, beaming from ear to ear.

AJ and I both stopped working and looked up. "A '57 Corvette?" AJ looked back at me and raised an eyebrow. A restoration like that would mean big money to the shop, depending on how much work it needed. He jogged back toward the office and disappeared inside the door.

Jillian chewed on her thumbnail as she watched him go. "Do you think you guys will be able to do it?"

"Shit, Jill, I think we'll have to make the time to do it, even if it's off hours. This is big."

She leaned against the car I was working on and looked at

the ground. "My dad would have loved this job." I lifted her chin until her eyes met mine. "He would have."

AJ barreled out of the office, clapping his hands and howling. "We got it, sis. He's bringing the car in next week so we can take a look at it." He grabbed Jillian in a bear hug that lifted her feet off the ground and swung her in a circle before letting go. "It's a huge job. We have to dismantle the engine completely. Fuel pump, carburetor, cylinder heads, and compressors—everything has to go. And that's just the start." He looked up at me with a huge smile. "You ready for this?"

"Definitely." I nodded.

"We're going out tonight. We gotta celebrate. It's tradition. You with us, brother? I couldn't have taken this job on without you."

"Hell yeah, I am!" I put my hand up and AJ high fived it.

"All right, man, let's finish up and get the hell out of here." We all scattered to get back to our jobs and finish out the day.

CHAPTER 13

Jillian

WE PULLED INTO Rhythm and Brews around eight o'clock, which was the time we agreed to meet. It was a bittersweet celebration, as it was our first one without Dad. I missed him so much, but I knew that wherever he was, he'd be so proud of the way AJ handled that call today.

I'd taken my time getting ready because I wanted this night to be special. The unworn dress I'd bought on a whim seemed like a good choice. The retro-style black halter clung to my figure all the way to the knee. Squeezing my rack into it was an interesting feat of strength, but I managed. Being under five feet tall with a solid D-cup was a cruel twist of fate. I had porn star tits and a twelve-year-old's ass.

The only shoes I owned were the red heels I wore to prom. Considering how crazy I went to find them, I was happy to be able to wear them a second time. Heels in my size were hard to come by, especially four inch ones. They were hard as hell to walk in, but they gave me a little height, so I didn't look like a pip-squeak in all the photos. Plus, I felt super-hot in them.

As AJ and I made our way inside, my eyes scanned the parking lot for Jameson's car, but I didn't see it. The huge bar in the center of the restaurant was packed, and pretty much every table around it was full. The hostess said it would be a few minutes, and AJ gave her his name. "I'm going to wait on the bench outside. You wanna come?"

"Nah, I'll stay here and wait," said AJ eying up an empty spot at the bar. "I'm going to grab a beer."

"Have fun. Call me when our table is ready." The night outside was beautiful. The setting sun turned the sky into a kaleidoscope of colors. Purple, orange, yellow, and blue curled around each other beyond the busy highway ahead. The sun is a powerful thing. It has the capacity to make or break us but still graces us with enough beauty that we give it our trust anyway.

Unfortunately, the bench full of smokers didn't share my sense of whimsy as they polluted the air with their stank-ass habit. I walked to the edge of the restaurant and leaned against the wall to enjoy my sunset alone.

The Mustang rumbled into the parking lot and my stomach somersaulted at the sight and sound of it. I smoothed my hands down my front and pushed the hair off my shoulders suddenly feeling self-conscience. I was too much of a tomboy to pull this look off; I shouldn't have tried so hard.

Jameson didn't see me standing there at first. Good Lord, he cleaned up nice. His button-down shirt was rolled up his wiry forearms just enough to see a few bold colors peeking out beneath the black cotton. It followed the contours of his broad chest and fell past his slim waist.

Much like the shirt, his dark jeans fit as if they were made for him. I was never one to swoon over dudes in nice clothes, but even dressed up Jameson still had a ruggedness to him. He was chiseled and strong and walked with a 'take no shit' swagger that I ate up with a spoon. I wiggled my fingers in a curt wave, and he smiled when he saw me standing there waiting for him.

"Hey, friend," he said, coming over to where I stood.

"Where's AJ?"

"He's inside having a drink at the bar."

Out of AJ's watchful eye, he placed his palm up on the wall next to my head and leaned close to my ear. The masculine scent of oil and spice assaulted my senses making my knees weak. "Are you trying to kill me or what?" The low baritone of his voice vibrated against my ear and the butterflies returned with a vengeance.

"What do you mean?"

"This dress, those shoes . . . how can I be expected to keep my hands off you when you look so fucking hot?" His forehead fell to mine and his fingertips grazed across my collarbone, lightly scratching the skin there. My body trembled, knowing all too well how skilled he was with those calloused fingers.

Our eyes met. The heat radiating between us was enough to melt the restaurant and everyone inside.

"I suppose it's an exercise in futility then, isn't it?" I replied.

He placed a kiss on my cheek and took a step back. "Shall we?" I linked my arm inside his waiting elbow.

AJ was leaned against the bar holding a draft beer when Jameson and I found him. "Hey man," he said greeting Jameson before turning back toward me. "The girl said it should only be a few more minutes."

The guys talked shop, and a nice man let me have his seat. I was thankful because while my fuck-me pumps were hot, my feet were already starting to hurt.

"Morello, party of three?" the hostess, an amazon-size redhead with legs for days, called above the noise of the bar. AJ raised his hand and left his empty glass on the wooden bar top as we followed her over to our booth. AJ slid in on one side and Jameson sat opposite him. I wasn't quite sure what the smart move was. I thought *what the hell?* and picked the seat next to Jameson.

When the waitress came by to take our order, AJ and Jameson ripped on me when they ordered beer and I ordered soda, but it was all in good fun. We ate and laughed and stayed long after our dishes had been cleared away.

The night wore on, and the waitress came by with a fresh beer AJ hadn't ordered. "Looks like you have a fan over there," she said, pointing at a slutty looking blonde at the bar.

AJ looked at her, then back at us with a shit-eating grin on his face. "Hold my calls," he joked, getting up from the table and strutting over to the girl, beer in hand. She twirled her over bleached hair and touched his bicep, laughing dramatically at whatever it was he said to her.

"I'm pretty sure we lost AJ," Jameson said, amused.

"I think you're right. He always did love the dirty chicks."

Jameson chuckled and inched a little closer, threading our fingers together under the table. "Never cared for them much myself."

Distortion came from the corner of the bar area as the band started to get ready to play their set. "Hey, everyone, we're Second Hand Flannel!" the singer shouted, and the opening chords to a Pearl Jam song started.

"Of course, they'd be alt rock," I grumbled and made a face. I was a self-imposed musical snob, and, sadly, the Seattle scene did not make the cut. My soul was much older than that and preferred its music raunchier and much less whiny.

Jameson snorted at my blatant distaste for the band. "You're terrible, you know that?"

"You say terrible, I say righteous and kickass!" I stuck out my tongue and winked.

I behaved myself for the next half hour, taking great pains not to point out the dude singing was actually reading the song lyrics off his iPhone while standing on the stage. AJ and his girl du jour were locked in conversation in the corner of the bar. She'd draped herself over him like a cheap suit, but he looked so happy that it made me happy by default.

Jameson's glass sat empty in front of him. Our tab was long since cashed out and the waitress was nowhere in sight. "I'm going to go up for another beer. You want another Coke?"

I shook my head and went in search of the ladies' room. There was a line. Of course. Maybe I was a horrible voice for my gender, but it always amazed me how long girls took in the bathroom. I mean, how long does it possibly take to pee and wash your hands?

The line moved as slow as peeling linoleum, but I finally made it inside and did my business before I burst used Coca-Cola all over the walls. After washing my hands, I slipped out of the ladies' room and was bumped by someone trying to go in. I stumbled on my too high heels and fell into another trashy looking blonde loitering in the hallway. The place was filled with them. "Excuse you," said the girl in what I'm sure was the bitchiest tone she could muster.

Righting myself, I turned to apologize, but words escaped me when I saw who she was with. Jameson's back was against the wall, and his arms were around Miss White Trash USA. "Excuse me," was the only thing my stunned brain could come up with to say.

I moved as fast as my heels would let me go. The place was packed, and I suddenly felt like I was going to suffocate from the confinement. I flew toward AJ and found him in the same spot with his girl. "AJ, I'm tired and this band sucks, give me the keys." I shoved my hand out, and he looked down at it confused.

Jameson was caught up in the thick horde of people standing around like cattle. Being able to sneak through crowds was one of the few times being little had an advantage. "Look, you can catch a ride with Jameson. Just give me the keys and let me go."

He fished them out of his pocket and dropped them in my hand. "I'll see you at home."

"Thanks," I shouted, as I made a beeline for the door.

My heels clacked along the concrete on my way to the truck. Jameson burst through the doors into the parking lot right behind me. "Jillian, wait! Stop running from me."

"It's okay, Jameson. We're cool. We never talked about being exclusive or anything, and I'm sure it's nice to be able to have a girl you don't have to hide, so no hard feelings on my part," I said, trying to sound apathetic as I opened the door and jumped in the seat. "Make sure AJ gets home safe. I don't want him catching the clap from Linda Lovelace in there." I slammed the door shut before he could say anything else and hit the lock.

"Jillian, c'mon!" He tried the door handle, but I turned the key and threw the truck in reverse, almost running over his feet as I skidded out of the parking lot like a bat out of hell. I peeked in my rearview mirror and saw him walking back into the bar.

"Don't cry, don't you dare cry," I said to myself. I cranked up the volume on the radio and tried to concentrate on anything else besides his hands on her skanky back. I was gone for, what, twenty minutes max, and he'd already found someone else? *That shit has to be a record or something.*

I peeled into the driveway praying there was beer in the fridge and cursing the fact that I had to see that jerk again on Monday. What we were doing wasn't technically dating, but I couldn't believe he would actually pick up someone else right under my nose.

Storming into the house, I kicked off my shoes taking my aggression out on them. They bounced off the wall and landed in a pile next to my sneakers. I wasn't even as angry with

Jameson as I was at my own naïvety. All his sweet talk was nothing but that—just talk, but I fell for it.

I ran upstairs and stripped off my dress before I even got to my room. A few hours ago, it was the nicest thing I owned, but now, I just wanted to light the damn thing on fire. My dad's old Dio tee was more my speed. I threw it on and went back downstairs to check out the beer situation. There were three left. I could work with that. I grabbed all of them, then parked myself on the couch hoping some mindless television would help relax me.

The sound of the front door woke me up. I was somewhere between awake and asleep and couldn't decipher if the heavy footsteps I heard were real or a dream. The blaring television became abruptly quiet. My eyes fluttered open, and I saw my brother tiptoeing toward the stairs. "AJ?"

He turned to face me. "Hey, Jill, I'm sorry I woke you. I didn't think you'd be on the couch."

I sat up and rubbed the sleep from my eyes. It was daylight out. "Are you just getting home? What time is it?"

AJ looked at his watch. "It's about nine a.m."

A sleepy smile curled along my lips. "Well, the bars close at two, so I guess this means you scored."

He looked at the carpet and scratched his head uncomfortably. "Yeah, well, what can I say? The ladies love me."

"Gross. Come sit by me." I yawned. He obeyed, coming to sit on the couch next to me. My legs curled up and my head rested on his shoulder. I missed the old AJ so much and I loved being able to catch this glimpse of him, short lived as it might be. "How'd Jameson do? Did Spray Tan Barbie have a sister?"

The deep rumble of his laugh vibrated in his chest. "No, Jameson left shortly after you did."

I sat up straight. "He did? Alone?"

"Yeah. Said he was ready to call it a night. Asked if I wanted a ride but Morgan had already offered to give me one."

"I bet she did," I said, snorting at my own lame joke. AJ just rolled his eyes and stood up.

"Glad to see you amuse yourself. I'm going to bed."

"All right, Fabio. Try not to get accosted by the ladies on your way up the stairs," I called after him. He dropped his face into his hand quick and ran up the stairs to go to sleep.

Jameson went home alone. *Well, that's interesting.* My palms reached toward the ceiling, stretching my sore muscles as I got off the couch. Knowing he didn't go home with the bathroom skank made me feel better, but I was still angry with the way everything went down last night. I needed to be smarter about things. This was a good thing actually. It's better I found out before I got too attached. Now, I didn't have to worry about AJ finding out anymore. I'd gotten it completely out of my system. At least, that was what I told myself as I walked into the kitchen in pursuit of a morning coffee.

Jameson

I SAT IN my car at Morello and Son's on Monday morning watching the clock. It was ten after eight, and she hadn't arrived yet. I had to talk to her. I wanted to go to her house after I left R&B's on Saturday, but I didn't want to risk AJ coming home and catching me there. That wouldn't have been good at all. If I had her number, I could have called her, but I wanted to talk to her face to face. The girl had the worst possible timing.

My gaze rolled toward the clock again. 8:20. *Shit*. She wasn't coming, was she? One hand raked through my hair while the other flicked at the stations on the radio. I messed this up. How could Jillian think I'd screw around with that piece of bar trash when I had her? There was no comparison between her and that chick she saw me with. She was a ten.

8:30. Dammit! My fist came down on the steering wheel. I was annoyed she didn't come early today and angry with myself for not having tried to talk to her sooner. I got out of the car and paced around in the parking lot in a vain attempt to stop stalking the clock. She would get there when she got there, and I'd talk to her. That was all there was to it. I kicked the gravel and sat on the trunk of the car.

Fuck. Fuck. Fuck.

I pulled my phone out of my pocket and checked the time again. 8:45. The office was opening in fifteen minutes; she should be coming any second. I jumped off my car and walked over to the front door of the shop. Keys tinkled and gravel crunched and my heart started hammering in my chest. "You missed our date," I said as she came around the corner.

"The fuck I did." She stood there glaring daggers at me, her arms crossed over her chest. "That ship has sailed, pretty boy."

"I'm sorry. It was a bad joke." I put my hands up in surrender. "Listen to me, Jillian. Saturday night was a case of bad timing, that's all."

"You don't need to explain yourself to me, *friend*. We had a little fun, but it's over now. Let's move on and go about our lives, m'kay?"

"Fuck that noise. That's bullshit and you know it." She flinched but held onto her resolve. She was a tough bitch. It was one of my favorite things about her. "I went to the bathroom looking for you. When I got there, your clumsy ass ricocheted off a fat chick and pushed that girl into me. That's *it*."

"Oh, yeah? How convenient! Can you explain why your arms were around her when I found you?" She pursed her lips and quirked her brow.

"I grabbed the girl just before she hit the ground. It was a reflex, nothing more. You stormed away so fast you didn't even have time to see the girl's boyfriend come up and grab her away from me. I almost got my ass kicked, I swear."

"Whatever." She rolled her eyes. "I admit it's a plausible sto-ry, but why don't we just cut to the part where this eventual-ly goes sour." She volleyed her finger back and forth between the two of us. "You know as well as I do that this can't last. Especially now that the business is doing so well. We can't risk AJ finding out about us and going ballistic. I need you in the shop more than I need you in my bed."

I moved closer to her calling her bluff. The fact that she didn't doubt my explanation, and she shouldn't 'cause it was true, told me all I needed to know. "You may need me in the shop, but you know you want me in your bed just as badly as I want to be there. Admit it, Jillian. Tell me right now that you don't lie awake at night thinking about me, and I'll walk into that shop and pretend anything you want me to pretend. I'll be your buddy during the day, do my job, and go home at night silently remembering the way your perfume clouds my brain, the way your smile lights up your face, and the way your breathy little moans sound just before you're about to come. Is that what you want, Jillian? Tell me. What's it gonna be?"

She looked up at me studying my face. She was trying her best to appear unflappable, but I could see it in her eyes. The fire. I could read it in her body language. The way she squeezed her thighs together when she thought I didn't notice. She was burning up just as much as I was.

We were mere inches apart. It was now or never. "Perhaps, you need a reminder." My lips crashed into hers with fury. Her hands came up to my face; I grabbed her ass and pulled her in tighter. It was crazy, AJ would literally be there any minute, but I couldn't go another whole day without touching her.

"You're right. I want you more than anything, but I'm scared, Jameson. I'm so scared." She placed little kisses all over my face then came back to my mouth.

"I'm never ever going to hurt you, Jillian. Look at me." I pulled away so she could see my face. She looked into my eyes; inside hers was a storm cloud of worry and lust combined. I said it again to make sure she heard what I was trying to say. "I'm never going to hurt you. Understand?" She nodded, and I pressed my lips to her forehead. "You're not getting rid of me that easily." I hugged her tightly then let go before AJ caught us for real.

CHAPTER FOURTEEN

Jillian

THE GUY WITH the '57 Corvette was scheduled to drop the car off on Friday mid-morning. Jameson and AJ worked like madmen all week to clear as much time in their schedules as possible to make room for the car in the shop.

Keeping with our routine, I opened the office on Friday at eight. I wasn't sure if Jameson would be coming or not, but the thought of him sitting there waiting for me made me too antsy to stay home. AJ got home late last night, and I was sure he and Jameson worked the entire time to prepare. I pulled out my chair and a hot pink sticky note was stuck to the seat covered in my favorite writing of all time.

There was a young guy with a Ford
He worked with a girl he adored
She was the star of his dreams
Sometimes dirty in themes
Because finding time alone together was hard
I miss you, cutie. Meet me at the pipeline tonight at 8:00.

With a sigh and a smile, I folded the silly poem and shoved it in my pocket. He left me a note, which means he wasn't coming this morning, but at least we'd get to spend some time together tonight. I definitely missed him too and couldn't wait to see him for more than five minutes in passing.

Around ten o'clock, a beat-up old Corvette sputtered into the lot followed by another car. Probably the guy's ride home. He was old, about sixty or so. I watched through the window as AJ walked out the bay doors to greet him. They talked out by the car for a long time then he gave AJ the keys and walked toward the office. The door buzzed as he walked in.

"Hello, dear," said the older man upon entering. He had an English accent and smelled of expensive cologne. "Mr. Morello sent me in to give you my contact information and leave a deposit for the work to be done on my car."

"Sure, no problem," I said smiling politely. A few clicks of my mouse, and the customer management software I used graced the screen in front of me. He and I did the usual dance back and forth, me asking questions and him answering them. When all was said and done, Randall Johnson III handed me the fattest deposit check I'd ever seen.

"Surely, you aren't old enough to be employed here regularly. You look like you should still attend high school," Mr. Johnson said as he took his receipt.

"Oh, well, thank you, sir. I actually graduated last year." I clipped a copy of the receipt onto the work order to keep everything together. "Okay, Mr. Johnson, you're all set. We will be in touch with you when your engine rebuild is complete."

"Wonderful, thank you miss . . ."

"Morello. But you can call me Jillian." I extended my hand in introduction and the man shook it gently.

"Ah, another Morello. The gentleman I met today would be your. . . . ?"

"My brother."

"Very nice. Rare you see a family business such as this these days." He winked and I smiled warmly as he said good-bye. Moments like that made me realize just how important keeping this place together really was. In a sea of Jiffy Lubes and Maacos, Morello and Son's Restoration stood alone and I was really proud of that.

$$\sim$$

AJ WAS STILL finishing up down at the shop when I was getting ready to meet Jameson that evening. I stood in front of the gaping maw of my closet in my bra and panties pondering what to wear. The old rock-n-roll tees I consistently wore hung in a neat row across the long rod inside, a rod lowered specifically for me. Almost everything I owned was a hand-me-down from my dad and totally worn to hell. Normally, I didn't care, but tonight, I wanted to look pretty.

I pushed aside shirt after shirt and stopped when I saw the vintage MTV tee I'd gotten from the Salvation Army. Pathetic as it was, it was the nicest one I had. My mind drifted back to the lust in his eyes when he saw me in that dress at the bar, and I fished out the only skirt I owned, a pleated denim mini. I fired off a quick text to AJ to let him know I was going out and locked the door behind me.

The pipeline was close by, and I made it there in no time. As usual, Jameson was already there waiting for me. The sight of his idling car triggered a reaction within me that could only be described as sheer delight. He saw me pull in and get out of the car. "Well, if it isn't my long-lost friend, Jameson Tate!" I joked as I jumped down from the truck.

"What can I say? I'm a busy man." He came around the car to where I stood and grabbed me in a hug that lifted my feet off the ground.

"So what's the plan tonight?" I asked as lowered me back onto the pavement.

He opened his passenger side door. "I dunno. Hop in. Let's go for a drive and see where it takes us." I slid into the bucket seat, and he closed the door. By the time he got into the driver's seat, I was already changing the CD. "You don't waste any time, do ya?"

"Lucky for you, I'm a girl who knows what she wants." I curled my legs up under me and settled back into my seat. Type O Negative bawled out of the dash and filled the interior with a demonic cloud of musical prowess.

Jameson shifted the car into gear, resting his hand on my bare thigh as he drove out of the lot. "Lucky, huh?" He glanced my way for a brief second flashing me that lopsided grin that drove me nuts.

I leaned over the stick shift letting his earlobe slide between my teeth. "Yep, very lucky," I whispered moving on to his neck. This afternoon's stubble was shaved away leaving his skin smooth against my face. I wasn't sure which look I liked better, but it didn't matter. Jameson looked good regardless.

The clean smell of his aftershave snaked its way around my body. I breathed him in and slid my hand between his thighs. "You're making it hard to concentrate on the road, cutie."

"Not nearly hard enough," I said rubbing the denim-covered semi-bulge through his pants. The breath hitched in his throat. I ripped open his fly and slid my hand inside. The car swerved, and his head fell back onto the seat as I stroked his length with my fingers.

"You're going to get us killed," he grumbled shifting in his seat.

"Are you asking me to stop?" My hand stilled, squeezing lightly.

"No friggin' way." He turned the wheel and got off the main road.

Simply touching him wasn't enough to satisfy my aching

need to please him. Jameson made me feel good in so many ways, and I wanted to return the favor.

I tugged his pants down just enough to expose him fully and dropped my eyes. His was the only dick I'd ever seen up close. Long, thick, and hard—it was exactly the way I'd pictured it.

A sudden bout of nervousness took hold as I wrapped my fingers around the base. Crippling self-doubt invaded my mind, but I pushed it aside, angled him up, and took him in my mouth.

"Fuck," he groaned. The steering wheel turned right next to my head, and he reached over my back to adjust the stick shift. Every vein and ridge pulsed against my tongue. I twirled it around the tip and his hand moved from the shifter to my head.

The haunting remake of "Summer Breeze" blasted loudly through the speakers. Jameson's ragged breath combined with Peter Steele's broody baritone sent shockwaves of need right through my core. I plunged my head again, taking as much of him into my mouth as I could, and using my hand for the inches I couldn't.

His hand was a fist in my hair now. Another breathy groan escaped his throat and a trickle of saltiness landed on my tongue. He throbbed in my mouth. I anticipated tasting his cum, but instead, I jerked forward as the car abruptly stopped and he pushed my head away.

Confused, I sat up in my seat and wiped my swollen lips. We were back at the pipeline again. He seemed like he liked it, so why did he stop me? "Did I do it wrong?"

"No, cutie. You did it perfect. Too perfect." He pointed his thumb toward the backseat of the car. "Get your hot ass back there. Now."

With a salacious grin, I crawled into the backseat. He tucked himself back into his pants and opened the door, having to move the seat forward to get in back with me. "You're insane. You know that, right?" I laughed, and he pulled me in. "You drive me crazy, Jillian. I don't know what you've done to me, but I just can't stop thinking about you. In my car, in my bed, in the shower, when I'm trying to fucking work. Your face is always on my mind. I just want you, all of you, all the time. Fuck AJ and his protective bullshit." He kissed me forcefully, as if he was sealing himself to me. "I want you to belong to me, Jill. Say you'll be mine."

"I'm already yours, Jameson, I always have been." I pulled him on top of me and leaned back on the seat of the car. The old leather squeaked under my weight as I shifted under him. He inched his hand up my skirt and pulled my panties down my thighs. It was awkward getting them off in the cramped backseat, but I managed to let my leg out one side. Jameson's pants were still unbuttoned from earlier, and I used my feet to slide them down just enough.

He reached back and grabbed a condom from his pocket. Just seeing it made me grow damp. I'd dreamed about this moment, and it was finally going to happen.

The foil glinted in the light of the street lamps across the way as he ripped the package open. He rolled the condom onto his thick erection and his lips claimed mine again.

The feeling of him at my opening made my palms grow sweaty and my heart race. So much wetness pooled between my thighs it was embarrassing. I was ready, and I wanted this so badly I could taste it.

As he started to push inside me, I winced and a tight squeaky whimper released from my throat. If I thought he felt big in my mouth, he felt colossal as he tore through my center.

A deep guttural growl vibrated against my lips, and his body stilled. "Jillian?"

"Yeah?"

He pushed himself up on his hands. "Is this your first time?"

He looked amazed, as if the idea that I might be a virgin never crossed his mind.

"Y-yeah," I stammered.

He sat up on his heels, ripping himself from me. "Why didn't you tell me you were a virgin?" He eyed me warily, the panicked look in his eyes was almost painful.

I pushed myself up on the seat next to him and clamped my knees together. "You never asked." I swallowed hard trying to ease the knot forming in my throat. "But it shouldn't matter. I want this. I want you."

He raked his hand through his hair hard and looked away from me. "But it does matter. What the fuck?"

Panic surged through me at the angry tone in his voice. "Jameson, please." The sound of my own voice was pathetic.

"I can't do this, Jill. It's all wrong." He started the arduous task of getting his pants back up in the confines of the backseat. I couldn't believe he was rejecting me again. All his sweet words and declarations fell to hell because of something as trivial as a hymen. I wasn't sure if I wanted to vomit or punch his face in.

Shame washed over me. I pulled my legs in and blindly searched the floorboard to find my underwear. "You're an ass-hole!" I spat, balling my panties up in my fist and fumbling the lever on the back of the seat to make it move forward. The faster I got out of that car and the further I got from him the better.

His long fingers wrapped around my arm as I flung the door open. "Come on, don't go."

I wrenched my arm from his grasp. "Don't you touch me. Don't you ever fucking touch me again." I jumped out of his car and ran over to the truck. He didn't follow me this time; he just got out of the car and watched me go.

How humiliating. I practically begged him to have sex with me and he refused. Everything he said to me was bullshit. If Jameson was playing a sick game to make me feel like shit, he'd succeeded. I felt worthless.

When I got back home, I sat in the truck in front of the shop trying to control the tears that wouldn't stop falling. I was full on ugly crying, and I couldn't go into the house like this. AJ would grill me about what happened, and I couldn't face him. He warned me to stay away from Jameson. I should have listened. He was right all along, and now, I've ruined everything.

IT WAS LATE by the time my tears dried up. I'd cried myself empty and there was nothing left but a gaping hole in my chest. I could still taste him in my mouth and feel him between my legs as I got out of the truck.

Blackness shrouded the area around the house as I slowly made my way up the walk. The lights were off inside, and I was thankful I didn't have to deal with AJ tonight.

I crawled into my bed in the dark and waited for sleep to take me, but it never did. Instead, I tossed and turned and watched the sun come up, passing out sometime around dawn. "Jill, are you getting up? It's almost nine," AJ said, knocking on my doorframe.

Too ashamed to even look at him, I didn't roll over. "I'm sick. I can't come in today."

"What do you mean you're sick? You were fine yesterday."

I pulled the covers up around me tighter, regardless of the summer heat. "I said I'm sick, okay? I'm sure the shop will survive my absence for a day."

"Whatever," he grumbled walking away.

I stayed in bed for a while longer hoping sleep would end the nightmare I was having while awake. I couldn't go back there and see him. After everything we'd been through, there was no turning back. I couldn't simply be his friend anymore. I was too far gone for that. As the second round of tears sprang from my eyes, I pulled the covers over my head hoping the heavy blanket would suffocate me.

Jameson

I WAS COMPLETELY destroyed when I got to work that morning. The look on her face when I told her we couldn't go through with it was etched in my memory. Her hateful words ran on a straight loop through my brain all night.

Why didn't I run after her and explain? I was an idiot, that was why. I promised I wouldn't hurt her, and that was exactly what I did. How could she not understand what I was trying to say?

I got to the shop after nine o'clock, and AJ was already there. I cursed myself, yet again, for being an asshole.

"You're late," he said as I walked in.

"Yeah, I know. I'm sorry; I'm dealing with some personal shit. It won't happen again." I walked over to the back computer to pull up the list of work orders for the day.

"It's cool, man, I get it. It's just Jillian is out sick, and we have a busy day ahead of us."

My hands froze mid-type. She didn't come in today. My mouth ran dry and my blood turned to ice. "What's the matter with her?" I tried to hide the feeling in my voice. I knew exactly what was wrong with her. She got involved with a jackass who stomped on her heart.

"I don't know, man. Probably woman shit." He walked over to the wall and smacked the button on the lift. My chest burned. The thought of her sitting at home miserable and cursing my name was excruciating. I had to get out of there.

The words jumbled on the screen when I pulled up the work orders. I couldn't concentrate on anything but getting back to her. Counting to ten, I closed my eyes and took a few deep breaths. When I opened them, the words on the screen made sense and I got to work.

The day was terrible. I made so many stupid mistakes that I was afraid to touch anything. "Dude, what's going on with you today?" AJ asked, after I spilled transmission fluid all over the place.

"I don't know, man. Just off my game. I got a lot on my mind." Red fluid trickled down the car and rolled over the concrete floor, I grabbed a rag and started to sop up the mess I made. "Would you be pissed if I skipped out at lunch, dude? I got some shit I gotta do."

He looked at me funny. He was a smart guy, and I'm sure it didn't pass by him that Jillian was sick, and now, I was leaving early for personal reasons. "Yeah, man, go ahead. I got this."

"Thanks, bro." I dropped the hood on the car and backed it out of the garage before getting into my own car and driving away.

Just as I'd done in the past, I went around the block and parked behind the house. The probability that she wouldn't hear me out was high, but I needed to try. She couldn't get rid of me that easily; I wouldn't allow it.

The house sat lonely among the trees as I ran through the shallow woods and up to the sliding glass door in the back. She was curled up on the couch watching television; a blanket laid half on her lap and half on the floor.

My stomach clenched as I tapped on the glass. She turned her head and saw me there, turning away in a huff. After the longest thirty seconds of my life, she got off the couch and walked over to the door. I swallowed hard, watching the graceful way she walked toward me, one naked foot in front of the other, arms swinging delicately at her sides. Her legs were bare and the tattered Anthrax tee shirt she wore was so faded you could barely tell the guy on the front was being electrocuted. It amazed me how she could be so hardcore, yet still so dainty at the same time.

She clicked the lock on the door and slid it open. "What do you want, Jameson?" she asked, the words sliding off her tongue like a razor. The look in her eyes tore me to shreds. It seemed like a lifetime ago that I kissed her dizzy on the table behind her instead of just a few weeks.

"Why aren't you at work?"

"I'm sick. What's it to you?"

I rubbed my bare arm with my hand, freezing under her cold glare. "We need to talk about last night."

"We have nothing to talk about. I'm so done with all of this. Go back to work." She turned her back on me, walking toward the family room, but I followed her inside. She stopped at the other end of the table and threw her hands up before letting them fall to her sides. "Why are you doing this to me?" Her shoulders rose and fell and her head hung low. I knew she was crying.

"Jillian, you need to understand."

"Understand what, Jameson?" She whipped around to face me. "The virgin won't be good enough in bed. Trust me, I heard you loud and clear."

I slammed my hands down on the table with such force that everything shook. "No! That's not it at all!" I shouted. "Don't you get it? You're *too* good!"

"*Too* good? What does that even mean?"

"You're too good for me, Jillian. Every day I see you and I can't believe someone like you can even like a guy like me. My own father didn't even want me. My mother killed herself just to get away from me. I'm nothing and you're everything, don't you see that? You're better than a quick fuck in the backseat of my car."

She stood there silent; her tear-filled eyes were saucers of surprise. "I'm really not that special," she said quietly.

My tone softened to match hers. "But you are. You're sweet and pure and beautiful in every way. You're selfless and kind. I'm less than zero. I'm a tumbleweed, a piece of dust, a pebble in the shoe of anyone I care about."

"How could you believe that? Stop saying you're nothing because you're not. I couldn't give a rat's ass about your parents, Jameson. You may have been nothing to them, but you're everything to me."

"You deserve so much more than I can give you."

"That's the problem. The only thing I've ever wanted is you." Another tear fell and I walked over and wiped it away. "Please kiss me." Her voice was barely a whisper. She looked up at me with her sad brown eyes, and it broke me. I wanted her too, so damn badly. Not just her body, *her.* Everything I'd told her last night was the truth. She changed me. She brought color into a life that was gray and bleak. I wanted to take her away from this shit life and give her everything she deserved.

I brought my mouth down to hers, and she kissed me hungrily, pressing her body against mine, not even caring that I was a mess from working all morning. "Take me upstairs, Jameson." Her leg came up around mine. I slipped my hands under her ass and hoisted her off the ground finally allowing myself to be sucked into the magnetic energy that had surrounded us since day one. I didn't have a pot to piss in. The only thing I could give her was the one thing I'd been denying her all along. The only thing I had to give. Me.

"Cutie, we can't do this until I've had a shower." I carried her up the stairs to the bathroom, setting her down on lid of the toilet as I reached into the shower to turn it on. She lifted her arms asking me to pull the old tee shirt over her head without having to use actual words. Her full tits rose and fell with each deep breath she took, but it wasn't even about that anymore. Not for me. This moment was going to connect us forever.

Steam began to fill the room. My hands skimmed her soft skin as the tee shirt fell away and landed on the floor. She followed my lead, sliding her hands under my shirt and pulling it off, searing her lips to my chest as it dropped to the floor next to hers.

Jillian fell to her knees, unbuttoning my pants and pushing them down. She looked up at me with a lascivious grin as my cock sprang free, maintaining eye contact as she slid her tongue from base to tip before standing up again.

I took her teasing little tongue in my mouth next and slid her underwear down her legs. My dick was so hard it was borderline painful, pressed against her taut stomach as she pushed her soft tits against me.

She stepped backward and pulled me into the shower with her. My fingers ran through her wet hair as the hot droplets of water rolled over her smooth skin. I grabbed a shower gel from the rack and squeezed it into my hand. The fruity scent that made me weak filled the tiny bathroom. "Citrus and Berries, huh?"

"Now, you know my secret," she said, scooping it out of my hand and lathering onto my skin.

"Your secret is my kryptonite." I pulled her under the hot spray with me. We washed and kissed and explored each other's bodies completely. It was hard not to pin her to the wall and have my way with her right there, but I forced myself to wait. I wanted to worship her in her bed like she deserved. We got out and I wrapped her in a big fluffy towel and carried her bridal style into her bedroom. The action was effortless; she was as light as a feather.

The bed dipped beneath our weight as I laid her down and

knelt next to her, dropping kisses over her wildly beating heart and trailing up to her mouth. Her body trembled. The towel fell open and my hand ran over her damp skin. There wasn't a single thing wrong with her. I'd seen her in various stages of undress, but seeing her bare and laid out in front of me, she was more spectacular then I'd dreamed. "You're amazing, Jillian," I said licking away a few remaining droplets of water that lingered around her collarbone, just like I wanted to do at that crappy motel down the shore.

My hands roamed over her breasts, teasing each nipple with my palm until they hardened into stiff peaks. Only after her whimpers became needy did I suck one into my mouth. Her hands buried in my hair and her thighs rubbed together stoking her own fire. "Jameson . . ."

I kissed a trail to her other nipple as my hand slid up her thigh parting her legs. My finger passed over her opening. "You're so wet for me already." I slipped it inside, and she constricted around it. I loved the way she enjoyed my touch. Ragged breaths rippled her exposed throat. Her head dug into the pillow, eyes pinched shut and hands twisting the sheets at her sides.

My lips moved down her body, raining kisses along her jaw, her chest, her stomach. The smell of her arousal scrambled my brain and made me ravenous. I nipped her thigh and nudged her with my nose before replacing my hand with my mouth. A keening cry ripped through the room as she clutched my hair in her fist. Her knees sprang up, and I spread them wider as I delved deeper into the sweetness that was all her. She was a heady mix of apples and sugar with her unique spice sprinkled on top. Jillian Morello was hands down my favorite flavor.

Heavy frantic breathing was all I heard as my tongue swirled and sucked. My finger found its way inside again, just one, but her walls clenched like a vise. So fucking tight. I groaned against her pussy just thinking about how fucking good it was going to feel gripped around my cock.

My finger crooked and teased her insides. I scraped my tongue hard against her. She began riding my face, a maneuver I'd grown familiar with. Her hips bucked, but I held her close. "Ohmygodshitmotherfucker . . ." She arched off the bed powerfully, blurting out a jumbled mix of curse words and moans, each and every one of them making my dick throb harder.

Her thighs clamped and her hand ripped at my hair, but I continued lapping up her sweetness as her body shuddered beneath me. Watching her come was quite possibly the greatest thing I'd ever witnessed. It was almost like an out of body experience. Her entire body convulsed with energy and her cute little mouth cursed like a sailor. If I had my way, I'd be seeing it over and over again.

"Jameson, I'm ready." She pulled me to her and my lips descended upon hers with fury. My knees knocked her legs apart and she accepted me between them, undulating her body against mine, covering me with her hot slickness. There was only one tiny detail standing in our way now.

Jillian came off the bed with me attached at the mouth when I tried to sit up to get a condom. "Shit, I left my pants in the bathroom." She reached out and pulled her bedside table drawer open. There was an unopened box just waiting for me. A big box. *That's hot.* "I love a girl who's prepared," I said, as I plucked it from the drawer. She giggled and pawed at my chest while I ripped it open and pulled out the foil wrapped condom.

I tore it open with my teeth and she yanked it from the wrapper and rolled it on me herself. Her hand stalled at the base of my shaft with a tender squeeze. I didn't just feel it in my dick; I felt it everywhere. She pumped once; her grip tightening and causing sparks to pop behind my eyelids. The reaction my body had to her hand was jarring. I settled down between her thighs again, knowing once I was inside her there was no going back. "Are you sure about this, cutie?"

"I've never been so sure about anything else, Jameson." Her breath on my ear and the sound of my name on her whispering lips was all I needed. I eased the tip into her, and she sucked in a hissing breath.

"Is it okay?"

"Mmmhmm." She sighed and drew her bottom lip between her teeth. I pushed myself all the way and groaned as she squeezed around me. I stilled for a minute, partly to allow her to adjust to the sudden fullness, but mostly because she felt so good I damn near passed out. She let out a series of squeaks at first, but they soon became moans as my languid rocking became steady and rhythmic. A fierce grind that sent her eyes rolling back and her nails digging into my skin.

Her hips began to move, and I let her set the pace. She was so tight and wet that I was finding it hard not to blow my load right there and embarrass myself, but I refused to come until she did. "Oh God, Jillian . . . Jillian . . ." Her name slipped off my tongue like a chant. I held her close, but I couldn't get her close enough. I wanted more of her, all of her. No other encounter had ever been this intimate. She made me feel like I was more than some dumbass grease monkey. I was needed, desired, cherished. In her arms, I felt like I actually mattered to someone.

Every noise she made was my reward. I pumped deep and fast reveling in her bliss and eagerness to take all I had to give. She wrapped her legs around my waist pulling me in. Our lips met in a tangled mass of wet kisses and slapping bodies. Nails dug into my back and her body tensed under mine. "C'mon, cutie, come for me again."

Another bundle of curse words bounced off the walls as her body spasmed and clenched around me. Hot wetness pooled between her thighs. I couldn't hold it in anymore. My climax nearly broke me. A guttural growl wrenched from my chest. My palm braced against the headboard, muscles strained as her body continued to wrack with pleasure.

I collapsed on top of her, drained and senseless, and she stayed wrapped around my body. Kisses covered my neck and shoulder. "I never want to let you go," she whispered into my ear.

"Then don't," I replied, kissing her as I continued to tremble inside her. I meant it. There was no way I was ever letting her let me go.

CHAPTER FIFTEEN

Jillian

"I'M GOING TO go take care of this."

Jameson slipped off the bed to go dispose of the condom. I watched his bare ass disappear into the hallway, hypnotized by the fluid way he moved and how all the muscles in his back seemed to ripple in the process. When he returned, he was back in his boxer briefs, carrying our clothes. He dropped them by the bed and laid back down next to me. My entire body felt loose and relaxed as I nestled back into his shoulder and captured his leg between mine. "What are we going to do about AJ?"

I sighed. "I don't know. He's just going to have to deal with it, I guess. When he comes home tonight, we'll talk about it."

"Nah, let me talk to him first. He'd respect that more," he said.

"Hmm, and they say chivalry is dead."

"Oh, I'm chivalrous all right," he said, rolling me to my back and pinning me beneath him. "I'll come in on my horse and ride you into the sunset and shit." His teeth nipped my shoulder and I giggled.

He leaned on his elbow resting his head in his hand. "Explain this to me." His fingertips grazed over the tattoo on my side.

"The two-headed flower is AJ and me. Just like us, they are two separate beings that share one root destined to be attached forever. The birds flying toward the clouds are my parents. The clouds part as they take flight allowing more sun to shine down on us. See the rays? Whenever I start to feel down, I look up toward the sky and think of my parents parting the clouds and forcing the sunshine in, helping us thrive."

"That's really beautiful. I'm glad you have nice memories to cling on to," he said getting serious.

"Tell me one of your nice memories."

"All the best memories I have include you." What started out as a chaste peck evolved into a passionate kiss that curled my toes. I couldn't get enough of him. He kneed my legs apart, melding his body to mine. Hardness pressed against me. My body reacted, heating up, getting wet, and wanting him inside me again.

Downstairs, the front door creaked open then slammed shut, and our heads whipped in the direction of the open bedroom door. "Shit," Jameson whispered. His eyes glanced at the clock on the table. "It's only three o'clock."

We scrambled off the bed throwing on our clothes as AJ's footsteps came up the stairs. I sent a silent prayer up above that he was going into the shower and not into my room to check on me.

"Jill, you awake?" His voice echoed out a split second before he materialized in my doorway. So much for the power of prayer. "What the fuck am I seeing right now?" His eyes squeezed shut as if seeing Jameson in my bedroom was a hallucination. "I fucking knew it!"

"AJ . . ." I started to say, but Jameson cut me off.

"Dude, let's talk about this. Man to man."

"I thought we had an understanding," AJ said, hands curled into fists at his sides.

"We did, and I tried to stay away from her man, but it's impossible." Jameson stood tall as I cowered behind the bed. "I'm crazy about her."

"That's unacceptable!" AJ's deep voice boomed out as he came further into the room. "I will fucking end you," he seethed through gritted teeth.

AJ raised his fist. I scrambled over the bed and jumped between him and Jameson. "AJ, stop!"

He looked at me as if he was possessed. I'd never sided against him in my life. The filthy trucker hat hurled to the ground. He raked his trembling hands through his raven hair and turned toward the door before spinning around and stomping back in. "Did you tell her?"

"Screw you, man," Jameson spat.

Both men came into my line of sight as I stepped to the side. "Tell me what?" I said, a queasy feeling in my stomach starting to take hold.

"Oh, of course, you didn't. You're not quite done with her yet." AJ crossed his arms ready to square off.

Jameson stepped to AJ chest to chest, glowering down at him. "You have no fucking idea what you're talking about. I suggest you shut your mouth before I shut it for you." Jameson's snarl terrified me, but AJ stood his ground. He was tough as nails and wasn't going to back down.

"You're not going to hit me, and you know it, bro." AJ's voice was deep and even but thick with warning.

"Uh, is someone going to tell me what the hell is going on here?" AJ wore a smirk on his face while Jameson looked like he was out for blood. My presence in the room was clearly forgotten, but inquiring minds needed to know right now.

Jameson's eyes glazed over, and AJ started talking. "She was fifteen, bro. How do you even live with yourself?"

"Who was fifteen? Jameson, what's he talking about?" My

heart was beating furiously.

"She had your fucking baby in her and you split like the piece of shit you are. You left her. Alone and pregnant." AJ's face twisted with disgust.

"You don't know the whole story, dude. It's not as simple as all that."

"Oh, it sounds pretty simple to me." AJ laughed cruelly. "You split and she couldn't deal. She killed herself. The end."

My back hit the wall with a thud, and I realized I'd been moving backward, away from this conversation. There it was. The big secret, and the reason for AJ's contempt. Jameson got some girl pregnant and ran away. "Why?" I said out loud. My brain was numb. Completely unable to fully process this information, I didn't know what else to say.

"Jillian, it's not what it sounds like," Jameson said.

"It's way worse than it sounds like," AJ seethed. "You fled like the irresponsible coward you are, then show up five years later and prey on my sister." Jameson reared back as AJ pushed him but didn't make a move to push back. "Why her?" AJ shouted, pushing again. "What was your plan, dude?" Jameson stumbled back as AJ's hands made contact with his chest a third time. "Use Jillian to kill time until you decide to split town again?"

"No man, it was never like that!" Jameson yelled.

"You could have had any girl you wanted, but you couldn't help yourself. You had to turn her into just another one of your whores." The cracking sound of Jameson's fist connecting with AJ's jaw made the bile rise in my throat.

"Don't you ever fucking call her that!" Saliva shot out through his gritted teeth, his gorgeous lips curled into a terrifying sneer. AJ spit onto my bedroom floor, and I was stunned by the redness in it.

I looked at him like a deer in headlights. Jameson's eyes were wild as he started toward me, but I put my hands up to stop him. "Let me explain." I couldn't tell if there was fear in his eyes or if I was just seeing my own fear reflected back at me.

"I can't handle this right now, Jameson. You need to go."

He shook his head and stayed put. "I'm not letting you throw me out again. You need to hear what I have to say about this."

My blood, cold at first, began to boil. I was furious at both of them. I'd been dragged into this series of lies and bullshit, and I never asked for any of this. The sight of them in my room was blinding me with rage so vibrant I was suddenly seeing things in Technicolor.

"And you!" My eyes fell on AJ as I clung to the wall for strength. "I'm so sick and tired of all your dominant male macho bullshit." My voice was shaking, but my tone was even and calm. "You come in here and start acting like a friggin' madman. Maybe you should have just been straight with me from the start instead of treating me like a child who couldn't handle herself."

"If you had done what you were told, it wouldn't have been an issue," AJ simply stated.

My calm exterior cracked, and I could feel myself losing control as my blood continued to boil from AJ's smug statement. *"Get the hell away from me! Now!"* I screamed. My ears were ringing from the sound of my own heart. Both men flinched, and I slid down the wall having exerted what was left of my energy.

"Jillian . . ." Jameson's voice pushed me over the edge, and I covered my face to hide the tears that had started to fall. AJ was right. I didn't know him at all.

"Just go," I whispered, as my body wracked with sobs.

Jameson turned and walked out of the room. "Good fucking riddance," AJ said as he passed.

"Get away from me," I said looking up at AJ. "I can't even look at you right now."

"*You're* mad at *me*? That's rich," said AJ with a humorless laugh. "Way I see it, I'm the only one taking care of their responsibilities right now. I'm down there working my ass off while you're in here fucking our employee."

"You don't have the right to talk to me like that!" My legs moved on their own as I jumped off the floor and ran full force at my brother. My body made contact with his strong build, and he staggered backward through the doorway of my room. I bounced off and fell to the floor again. Pain radiated up my tailbone. I grimaced, and AJ's face filled with pity. "I hate you right now."

"Whatever." He turned away from me and walked down the hall. The front door slammed a few minutes later. I was alone again. I hugged my knees close to my body on the floor, confused and unsure of everything that had happened that day. How could I believe anything Jameson had said to me in the past was the truth? He looked my brother in the face and lied effortlessly so many times; there was no reason to think he wouldn't do the same thing to me.

I was a fool who let my stupid heart get in the way.

I crawled back into my bed. It was cold without him there next to me. I missed him already, and I hated my body for betraying me like that. Why the hell couldn't all of the parts of me work together in unison? I was torn between what was right and what I wanted, and I was so exhausted from dealing with it.

Just when I'd actually chosen a side, the rug was ripped out from underneath my feet and I hit the ground face first. I tried to picture Jameson being so heartless, but I just couldn't imagine it. His eyes reflected nothing but kindness. His hands, while rough to the touch, were always so tender whenever they handled me. I had to talk to him about it. My mind was telling me to forget him and move on, but my heart was telling me to listen to what he had to say. After everything we'd been through,

I owed him that much.

I fell into a deep sleep and dreamed of Jameson. His beautiful face was twisted into an angry snarl, and he was punching bags of flour. The white dust was flying everywhere suffocating me. It filled my nose and mouth and caused my eyes to sting. I was trying to cry out to him to ask him to stop, but he just kept pounding them over and over.

Banging on the front door startled me awake. I rolled over and looked at the clock. AJ stormed out six hours ago.

"Hang on!" I yelled, as I padded down the steps to see who the relentless caller was. I threw open the door, shocked to see the police on my stoop. "Can I help you?"

"Is this the home of an Anthony Morello Jr.?" He looked down at his little pad as he said my brother's name.

He's been arrested. He found Jameson and started a fight, and now he's in jail. "Yes, he's my brother. What's happened, is he okay?"

The cop took the hat off his head and began turning it in his meaty hands. His hair was thinning on top. His face would have been completely unmemorable if not for his piercing blue eyes. "Can I speak with your parents, miss?"

"They are dead, sir. Where is my brother?" The way his eyes turned soft and filled with remorse made me ill. He couldn't even look at me. Goose bumps covered my skin as I waited to hear what the officer had to say. Panic started to rise in my throat for the second time that day.

"There's been an accident."

CHAPTER SIXTEEN

Jillian

MY BLOOD WAS ice. The house spun. My stomach dropped. The uniformed man on my porch became a blur. Then . . . vomit.

"Miss, is there someone I can call?" I sat back on my haunches at the sound of the cop's question. The roller coaster of today's emotions culminated with me dry heaving in front of my childhood home, the puddle seeping into the ground in front of me hitting home that this was real and not a horrible dream. There was literally no one he could call. AJ was all I had left in the entire world.

"No. I'm fine now. Take me to him. I'll go get my stuff." I wiped my mouth and rose to my feet. My throat burned, and my legs were weak, but it took me no time at all to run inside and grab what I needed before meeting the cop out front on my porch again.

Having never been inside of a cop car before, it was weird. I felt like I'd done something wrong. The ride seemed to take forever, and my nails were slowly being chewed to the quick as the streetlights on the highway rushed past. We pulled up in front of Crestmere Hospital and the cop escorted me into the emergency wing. "Anthony Morello Jr.," I said to the woman behind the desk. She tapped on her computer and picked up the phone.

"Have a seat. The doctor will be right with you," she said replacing the receiver on the hook.

The uncontrollable bounce of my knee shook the carpeted floor beneath my feet. My hands wrung in the hem of my shirt and the coppery taste of blood filled my mouth as I bit at my lips with anticipation. If I thought the ride here was long, the wait seemed endless.

A young looking man in blue scrubs walked into the waiting area scanning the room. "Morello?" he said.

I scrambled out of my seat. "I'm Jillian Morello. Where's AJ? Can I see him?"

The doctor extended his hand, and I shook it. "I'm Dr. Walters. I'll take you back to see him in just a minute. He was hit by a drunk driver who ran a red light." The doctor demonstrated the accident by using his hands. "Your brother's car was hit on an angle. The other car careened into him hitting him here, in the backseat. He's extremely lucky the car didn't make contact with the driver's side, but the angle of impact forced his seat forward and pinned him between the seat and the steering wheel. He suffered a dislocated shoulder, two broken ribs, and some moderate head trauma. We are still running tests, but he's been placed in a medically-induced coma to reduce any swelling of the brain."

The doctor's forensic recount of AJ's accident left me numb. He led me into the emergency room. The strong smell of antiseptic burned my nose and made my eyes tear. Along the long wall, curtained off rooms all contained patients injured in various ways. We walked past several of them before the doctor stopped in front of one.

My brother lay motionless in the bed hooked up to all kinds

of wires and tubes, while machines behind him beeped in unison. His head, torso, and right shoulder were wrapped in bandages. AJ's usually stocky form seemed so helpless and small. The context of our last conversation passed through my mind. I told him to leave me alone, that I couldn't stand the sight of him.

I told him I hated him.

A lump formed in my throat when I realized how trivial it all seemed right now. I sat in a chair next to his bed and took his big hand in mine. His hands were rough and the skin around his fingernails stained from years of working in the shop. I never noticed before, but he had the same hands our father did.

"AJ, I don't know if you can hear me. I'm here, and I'm sorry." I laid my head on his arm and listened to the steady rhythm of the machines, feeling so alone. For all the tragedy I've seen in my life, I'd never had to do it by myself. AJ was always by my side. Now, he was on the other end, and I wasn't sure if I had the ability to be strong without him. We shared a root. Surely, once he wilted, it wouldn't be long before I did too.

The doctor let me stay there for a long time just sitting with him, but eventually, the time got late and I was forced to go. I was a zombie just going through the motions. The nurse came in with AJ's belongings and dropped them in my lap. *What do I do now?* I was stuck there. I'd come with the police officer and didn't have any relatives to call to pick me up.

The hard rectangle of AJ's phone knocked against my hand, and I fished it out. There was only one other person who I could think to call. My mind raced trying to come up with anybody else who could possibly come get me. I had a couple of girlfriends, but since school ended, we weren't all that close anymore. I sighed heavily and pressed send.

Jameson

I WAS SITTING in my room torturing myself with the disastrous events of the day over and over again. It was late when my phone rang, and I was shocked to see AJ's number. It made me nervous. My first thought: either something happened to Jillian or he was drunk and calling me to fight.

"AJ, what's up?" There was nothing on the other end at first, and I assumed he'd butt dialed me or something. A faint weepy sound filtered through the earpiece. "Jill?" The crying escalated, and my heart hammered in my chest. Something was very wrong. "Jill. Where are you? What's wrong?"

"He promised he was never going to leave me." She managed to get out between sobs.

"Who did? Where are you? Where's AJ?" Her voice sounded hollow and her riddle terrified me beyond belief. I threw on my shoes and frantically searched the room for my keys.

"Crestmere Hospital."

"I'm on my way. Just sit tight and wait for me." Keys in hand, I ran to my car and jumped in.

I raced to the hospital probably breaking a hundred traffic laws in the process. The car screeched into the lot and I found the first available spot. It was far from the door, so I sprinted to the emergency room exit. My chest burned. The automatic doors opened. I bolted toward the hospital desk. "Morello," I choked out between gasping breaths.

"Jameson?" I whipped around when I heard her meek voice behind me. Her face was puffy and stained from tears. She was clutching a bag of something in her arms like it was a lifeline. She was a total mess, but the sight of her standing in front of me, not lying in some hospital bed, was the most beautiful thing I'd ever seen. Her knees buckled when I pulled her against my chest and fresh tears shot out of her eyes.

"I'm here, cutie. I'm right here." Damp strands of hair stuck to her cheeks and forehead. I smoothed it back, dropping my lips in their place. She collapsed into an empty chair. The bag fell from her arms. "What happened? Talk to me," I said, kneeling in front of her and taking her freezing hands in mine.

Her soulful eyes were red and drowning in tears. "AJ had an accident in the Firebird." She hiccupped. "Some fucking drunk driver came out of nowhere and T-boned him in an intersection."

I wiped her face with the sleeve of my sweatshirt jacket. "Where is he now?"

"He's in a medically-induced coma." Her skin was ice cold. I shucked off my jacket and rested it on her shoulders. "I'm sorry. I just didn't know who else to call."

She crumpled like a sheet of tissue, and I took her in my arms again. "Don't apologize. I'm here for you, always. No matter what.

"Come on. I'll take you home." She slipped her arms into the jacket and wiped her face with her cotton-covered hands. I put my arm around her shoulders and steered her toward the door. She walked to the car and dropped lifelessly into the passenger seat.

The ride home was silent. She didn't mess with the radio or say a single word, but she'd stopped crying, so that was progress. When we got to the house, I practically had to carry her inside. She kicked off her shoes and flopped onto her bed like a rag doll. I covered her up and sat next to her on the edge. "Get some sleep," I said rubbing small circles into her back.

"Please don't leave yet." She curled up on her side in the fetal position. Her body looked like a tiny lump in her bed. "Will you lie with me until I fall asleep?" Her voice sounded so small, like she was a million miles away. I switched off the light on the nightstand and laid next to her as she'd asked.

Even after she'd fallen asleep, I stayed there holding her tight. I couldn't bring myself to leave her all alone. Truthfully, I was scared to death. I didn't want to think about what would happen to Jillian if AJ didn't recover.

It wasn't an option.

They needed each other.

Her body thrashed around in the bed. I startled awake, unsure what the hell was going on. I didn't even remember falling asleep. "Jillian." She was soaked in sweat and tears. I shook her lightly trying to wake her up. "Jillian, you're having a bad dream." Her entire body shook like a leaf, clinging to me for dear life. "It's okay. I got you."

Her leg hooked around my waist and her lips danced along my neck. "Hey. Hey," I said softly. "Just relax, you're all right."

"I'm not all right." She sniffled. "I feel like I'm suffocating. Whenever I close my eyes, he's all I see. It hurts so badly."

"I don't know how to help you, Jill."

"Just make the pain go away. Even if it's for just a little while, I need to feel something other than this." Cold lips devoured mine, salty tears bled into our joined mouths. She was out of her mind with grief. Jillian didn't want me; she wanted a distraction. There was no affection behind her embrace; it was determined and depressing.

The situation was lose-lose for me. Either I took advantage of her pain and mercy fucked her mindless, or I rejected her when she needed me most. Either way, the result would be the same and I'd end up looking like an asshole.

"Please, Jameson." She pushed me onto my back, her little body covering mine, biting at my skin and taking what she needed.

It was wrong on so many levels. I should have told her no and put her back to bed, but I just couldn't do it. She needed a temporary release from this tragedy, and I was the only one who could give it to her. I laid back and let her take it out on me as many times as she needed to until sleep finally took her for the night.

CHAPTER SEVENTEEN

Jillian

JAMESON AND I were still tangled up in each other as the summer sun started to shine through the windows of my room. He gave me what I needed, many times over. I was grateful for the diversion, but the light of morning served as a reminder it was time to be a grown-up and deal with this bad acid trip I called my life.

My gaze dropped to his sleeping face in my bed. What was his motive here? I called him in the night and he ran to me no questions asked. He kissed my tears and whispered sweet words into my ear as he moved inside me. The idea that he could potentially disappear like a thief in the night twisted a knife deep in my gut. I didn't know what I'd do if I woke up and found him gone, but I couldn't take the risk and put myself in that position. AJ was my first priority now.

I scrawled a note to Jameson on a sheet of scrap paper and left it on the pillow next to him. My big loopy letters were the antithesis of his tiny neat ones.

Thanks for last night. See you around. -J

As quietly as I could, I put myself together and mentally

prepared myself to see my brother.

It was early and the hospital was quiet. I got to the reception desk and wondered if it was too early for visiting hours. "Morello," I said approaching the lady sitting at the desk.

She tapped on her computer and paused as she read the screen. "Anthony?" she said. My skin crawled at the sound of my father's name. It was my brother's legal name too, but no one ever used it. I nodded and she handed me a pass with a room number on it.

"Where is this?" I asked taking the pass. She gave me directions to the ICU. I thanked her and walked down the hall of the hospital. *He was moved to a room. That had to be a good sign, right?*

The nurses' station in the ICU was empty. I looked around but didn't see anyone. I found the room by myself and walked in. He looked exactly the same as yesterday and my hopes deflated. I didn't know why I expected a dramatic change. Just wishful thinking, I guess.

"Hi, AJ. I'm back." I pushed a dark wave of hair off his forehead as I whispered to him. "Please be okay. I promise I'll never see him again if you just wake up." I sat in the seat next to his bed and waited. It was quiet on the floor except for the slight hum and beep of machines and the sound lulled me to sleep.

Rustling in the room made my eyes flutter open. A nurse was checking AJ's equipment. I stretched trying to relieve the aching pain in my back and neck from the stupid chair. "Hello there," said the nurse. "Friend or family?"

The nurse didn't seem like she was much older than AJ. She was blond and perky and her scrubs had puppies all over them. "Family. I'm his sister."

"Well, I'm the day nurse. My name is Beth." She pointed to a chalkboard on the far wall with her name and shift times written on it. "If there is anything you need, just ring the station."

I was well versed in hospital customs. Ringing the station

took a night and a day to get anyone in here; it was easier to take care of everything myself. I'd taken care of AJ for years; there was no reason to stop now. "Thanks, Beth. Is there someone I can talk to who can give me an update on his condition?"

Beth looked at her watch. "Dr. Rumson should be coming by in about an hour. She'll be able to answer any questions you have."

"Okay, thanks. I'm going to get out of your hair and grab something from the coffee shop downstairs." I rubbed my eyes and walked out of the room. The waiting game was the worst part of all of this. Our mom clung hopelessly to life for weeks, and there was nothing for us to do but sit and watch.

If only I had a machine that I could use to go back to Saturday afternoon and start over. I would tell Jameson to leave my house and go back to work and none of this would have ever happened.

The thought stopped me in my tracks. The shop. I was so beyond worried about AJ that I hadn't even considered what was going to happen with it now. Fixing cars was so far out of my area of expertise it was laughable. The only option was to close the place down until further notice. It would result in an absurd loss of money, money we desperately needed now to cover our portion of the medical bills, but I had no other choice.

The deep rumble of my name echoed through the lobby as I neared the coffee shop. *Shit.* I turned around and Jameson was jogging in my direction. He pulled my crumpled note from his pocket. "You wanna explain this shit to me?" His voice was calm and low, but the anger shone through his dark green eyes.

I shrugged. "What's to explain? You helped me out last night, I said thank you, and now your job is done. I don't need you to be here anymore. I'm fine."

His eyes narrowed. "You're unbelievable, you know that?

Yesterday you were all over me, and today, you treat me like I'm a disease. After everything that's happened between us, you're going to push me out of your life now? For what? A mistake I made five years ago?"

I pinched the bridge of my nose with frustration. "I don't have the time or energy for this right now. What do you want me to say? It was fun. We both got it out of our system and it's time to move on. Now, if you'll excuse me, I need to get back to my brother." I tried to walk past him, but he stepped in my way.

"You wanna feed me that line again? Fine. But I'm not going anywhere."

I rolled my eyes. "What can I do to get you to leave right -" His mouth dropped to mine with a force that almost knocked me over. My traitorous body responded, pressing against him as my hands found their way into the silkiness of his hair. After everything that happened in the last day, I still wanted him, but it was time to start making decisions with my head instead of my heart. I chose the latter once, and look where it got me.

Savoring the moment one last time, I sucked his lips into my mouth, committing his taste, his smell, and everything I loved about kissing him to memory before backing up for good. "Good-bye, Jameson."

I walked into the cafeteria and ordered myself a coffee and a bagel, pretending not to notice Jameson loitering out in front of it. When I returned to AJ's room, he followed. He didn't say anything to me, just stayed a few steps behind and sat in a chair just outside his door.

Settling into the chair cross-legged next to AJ, I sipped my coffee. "Don't worry about the shop, dude," I said to his lifeless body. "I'm going to go in tomorrow morning and make a few calls, reschedule appointments. Everything is going to be fine there. I can hold down the fort. You just concentrate on getting better." I didn't know if he could hear me, but I remembered reading somewhere that it was recommended that people speak and act just like they can. Besides, me blabbing on and AJ staying quiet was pretty commonplace for us.

"The Firebird is wrecked, but I'm sure you know that. It's cool, though, because I know a great mechanic. As soon as he wakes up . . ." I trailed off finding it difficult to speak. My throat felt like it was going to close up. I didn't want him to hear me crying. He needed to think everything was fine, so he could concentrate on getting better instead of worrying about me. The rapid-fire blinking of my eyelids cleared away the wetness, and I took another swig of my coffee.

There wasn't much to say after that. I just sat in silent prayer watching his chest mechanically rise and fall. Out in the hall, a pair of long legs and work boots sprawled out.

I wanted to be annoyed that Jameson was still there, that he hadn't listened to me and just gone home as I'd asked. He was so damn stubborn, and I should be angry, but I wasn't. He cared for AJ, and he belonged here. Their last conversation was less than loving as well. I hadn't considered that he might be hurting, but I was too selfish to let him in. It was too hard for me to turn off my feelings for him, and I had to keep my distance.

A woman with caramel colored skin and short black hair came in. She pulled the chart on the foot of AJ's bed and adjusted her glasses as she read it. "Are you Dr. Rumson?" I asked standing from my chair. "I'm Jillian, AJ's sister. Can you tell me what's going on with him?"

She flipped through the chart and read before answering my questions. "Your brother has suffered a brain contusion and a slight skull fracture."

"A brain contusion, what is that exactly?"

"Simply explained, a brain contusion is like a bruise of the brain tissue. When the body moves in one direction at a certain speed then suddenly comes to a stop, the brain continues to move within the skull in that direction, causing it to bounce against the hard skull, damaging that area of the brain."

My mind conjured up this image of a tiny silver brain bouncing from wall to wall inside a giant skull shaped pinball machine. "So his brain is bruised? How badly?"

"Contusions could be very minor or quite severe, depending on impact. The good news is that your brother isn't the worst case I've seen, but the bad news is the swelling of the brain is a little more substantial than we originally thought. We will need to keep him in the medically-induced state for the time being and continue to monitor him to see if it starts to come down."

"What happens when it comes down?"

"If the swelling begins to subside, we can slowly stop the drugs and he will begin to wake up shortly after."

"And if it doesn't?" I was smart enough to deduce the answer to that question myself but I needed her to spell it out for me.

"If intracranial pressure remains high, it can prevent blood passage, which results in further brain injury and eventual death." I had been expecting it, but the candid way the doctor dropped the D word knocked me off my feet and back into the chair behind me.

AJ could die.

I'd feared it, but hearing it out loud made it just that much more real. The bile rose in my throat again, like when the officer showed up at my house. I willed myself to calm down and not lose my bagel all over the doctor's loafers. "In the meantime, we will do frequent CT scans to monitor him as much as possible and hope for the best . . ."

The doctor continued, but I'd stopped listening at that point. The only thing I could hear was my own heartbeat thrumming in my ears. My chest hurt. I couldn't breathe. My tongue was thick, and my palms were sweaty. The doctor became a blur in front of me as the room began to spin. I clutched my throat and tried to suck in as much air as I could, but I felt like I was trapped in mud. "Jillian, breathe."

The doctor's voice sounded faraway, like it was coming through a tunnel. Her hand rested on my back, and I tried to copy her breathing in front of me. I felt a second hand on my back, a much larger one. "Breathe in one . . . two . . . three . . . four. And out." The doctor exhaled, and I followed. "Good, good. Keep going."

Slowly, the room stopped spinning, and I started to see more clearly. The doctor's eyes glanced behind me then back to my face. "Keep breathing." She stood up and retrieved a cup of water from the bathroom. "Does that happen often?"

"Does what happen often?" I reached for the cup and took a drink.

"What you just experienced was a panic attack. I can write you a script for something if you think you need it."

"No, no, I'm good. Thanks." I took another sip of the water, and the doctor's eyes flickered over my shoulder again. The large hand left my back and heavy boot-laden footsteps walked back out into the hall.

The doctor scribbled down something on her little blue pad and handed it to me. "Well, here, take it in case you decide you need it. It's very mild." I took the square of paper from her hand and looked over at my brother. The doctor excused herself and walked out of the room; while out in the hall, the same denim-clad legs and work boots quietly waited along with me.

Jameson

I SAT IN the hallway all day while Jillian just waited by AJ's bed. She told me to go home, but forget that, I'm not leaving her to deal with this all alone. She never had to be alone again. AJ was right on the money when he said she threw on a tough exterior. If she wanted to play that way, that was cool with me, but I wasn't going anywhere.

It was late in the evening when I peeked into the room. She was curled up in the chair next to him with her head on the armrest, fast asleep in spite of the coffee cups that littered the table next to her. She was exhausted. "C'mon, Jill. Let me get you home."

She lifted her head to look at me then dropped it back onto the armrest. "I can't go. He needs me here."

"He needs you to be strong for him. You can't do that if you don't get some rest. You've been here all day, and he knows." She sat up, her groggy face turned down in a sad pout. I hated seeing what this was doing to her.

"I'll see you tomorrow." She dropped a quick kiss on AJ's forehead then turned and left his room. We maneuvered through the hospital and out into the parking lot, me trailing just a couple of steps behind her, giving her the space she requested earlier. I didn't want her to drive but decided it wasn't worth the fight she'd ultimately put up when I suggested that. Instead, as she pulled out of the parking lot, I followed behind making sure she got home safe.

We pulled into her driveway, but she didn't make a move to get out of the truck. I waited for five minutes or so before getting out of my car and approaching her. "You all right?" I asked through the open window.

She was sitting in the idling truck looking down at her hands on her lap. "The whole car ride home, I imagined pulling into the lot and seeing the lights in the shop on. I'd pull up to the house and his stupid blue car would be sitting off to the side like it always was. But the lights are off and the car is gone and the house seems so dark. My entire family is gone. I'm as empty and lonely as that house, and I'm afraid if I go inside, the darkness will swallow me whole and I'll never see the sunshine again."

I couldn't say anything that would make her feel better. I opened the car door, reached inside, and pulled the keys from the ignition. Inside the house, I jogged around turning on every single light in every room before heading back outside again. The windows lit up the wooded area surrounding her house and cast a bright light onto her sad face through the truck windshield. "I can never replace your family. But I can promise that you'll never have to face the darkness alone."

I pulled her from the truck and walked her inside the house hand in hand. She settled onto the couch and pulled her legs up under her like she always did. The bagel she had was hours ago; she needed to eat something.

Rifling through the fridge, I found what I was looking for. I wasn't much of a cook but managed to throw together a mean grilled cheese sandwich. "Eat," I said, holding the plate out for her when it was done.

"Thanks." She took the plate and set it down on her lap. I sat on the couch at the opposite end while she picked at the sandwich. "Aren't you eating?" she asked in true Jillian fashion. She was always so damned concerned about everyone else that she never stopped to worry about herself.

"I'm good." We sat in silence watching some home decorating show on HGTV while she nibbled on her dinner. When the plate was empty, I brought it back into the kitchen and loaded everything into the dishwasher. I joined her again with a bottle of water and set it on the couch next to her. "I am going to run to my place for a minute and get some stuff, but I'll be back."

She nodded. All the fight had gone out of her. I had no idea what tomorrow would bring, but for today, she was letting me take care of her for a change. For as long as I could remember, I'd only had myself to worry about. Caring this much about another person was something I'd never had to deal with before.

I grabbed the blanket from the back of the couch and wrapped it around her slim shoulders. I hated leaving, but I needed clothes and a real toothbrush. This morning, I'd used toothpaste and my finger, and that shit was not going to work long term.

Her reaction to AJ's prognosis scared the shit out of me. The sound of her gasping for breath like a fish out of water was terrifying. I admit it was hard for me to keep from losing my own shit when I overheard the doctor, but I need to keep it together for Jill.

She may not think so, but she needs me.

CHAPTER EIGHTEEN

Jillian

I WOKE UP in my bed in the middle of the night. The last thing I remembered was passing out on the couch while potential homebuyers on HGTV whined about lack of closet space. Jameson must have come back and carried me to my bed.

The lonely feeling in my gut returned. I sat up in the dark, wondering if he'd gone home. The low hum of the television played in the distance as I walked down the stairs giving me my answer.

"Couldn't sleep?" he asked, as I walked over to where he was. He lifted the blanket and I crawled under it next to him, the warmth of his bare skin surrounding me as we spooned on the couch.

"No. Can't turn my mind off." His strong arm fell over me and I could feel his heartbeat on my back. "I am trying to stay positive, but it's not easy. The Morello family track record for recovery is for shit." He squeezed me tighter.

I wriggled my body around until I was facing him. Our legs tangled and his thick fingers trailed through my hair as I snuggled under his chin. It was so easy to control myself while the sun was out, but the nights were more difficult. The only time I felt a comfortable reprieve from my own horrible thoughts was in his arms.

I grazed my fingertips up and down his strong back and his contented sigh dared me to continue. My hands snaked around to the peaks of his chest and skimmed down the deep channels of his flawless abs. They clenched under my touch as I slid my hand into the waistband of his boxers.

"Jillian, you should try to get some rest," he whispered hoarsely.

"Rest is overrated." I rolled him on top of me and tried to kiss him.

He propped himself up on his elbows just out of my reach. The dim light of the television flickered in the background casting a haunted glow on his face. "Am I really what you want?"

"Right now, you are." My back stretched up to reach him, and my lips found his neck. There was no way of knowing how I'd feel in the morning, but one thing was certain. I was at constant odds with myself and didn't want to make promises to another man I cared about that I knew I couldn't keep.

His body tensed with hesitation. I dropped back down to the couch and wiggled my shirt up over my head, dropping it onto the floor. "Are you going to make me beg you again?"

Desire and conflict swirled in his eyes as they wavered over my naked torso. His soft lips made contact with the skin over my heart and his hands clutched my back as he kissed his way up to my mouth.

My leg draped on the back of the couch. The soft cotton of my underpants was damp and he groaned as he pressed himself against them. Every time our bodies touched, roiling embers singed my skin, fueling my need for more, but right now, I needed to feel all of him to drown out the other feelings that were bubbling to the surface.

I hooked my thumbs into his boxers and pushed them down as far as I could before using my feet to get them the rest of the way. Getting my own off wasn't nearly as easy. "Patience is a skill you've not acquired, is it?" he teased.

The slow way he pulled my tiny briefs off was torture. His eyes burned into mine as he shimmied them off my legs trying to take back a little control of this situation. "I prefer my gratification instant," I said, reaching for his cock and guiding him to my center.

Jameson was always so careful with me, so loving and tender, but tonight, I wanted wild and rough. I needed him to help me forget, to pound out the thoughts that infested my mind like roaches.

I hooked my leg around his backside and pulled him in. He thrust hard, and we both moaned simultaneously. My body returned from the depths of despair and started to come alive again. Every nerve ending in my body popped like cherry bombs in a fire. I bit and sucked and scratched at his skin as I writhed beneath him, taking out my aggression and jerking my pelvis up to his at a furious pace.

The sweet sensation of climax slithered across my tailbone and churned in my stomach. "Go harder and don't stop," I pleaded. He continued to tear into me, grunting with exertion but all I heard was the sound of my own mangled scream as I came. "shitshitshit . . ." I panted and shouted as another orgasm directly followed the first one.

Drenched in sweat and out of breath, he slowed his hips and my eyes rolled back in my head. My body quaked from deep within. Every synapse in my brain fired in opposite directions, and for a brief glorious moment, I'd forgotten everything and everyone except for him and sheer euphoric pleasure.

"It's okay, baby, It's okay," he whispered into my ear, his soothing voice bringing me back to the surface of reality. I touched my face, and it was wet. Salty tears leaked from my eyes and rolled into my ears.

My arms and legs wrapped tight around him as he moved within me. "Just don't stop. Don't ever stop," I murmured over and over.

The next thing I recall was the sound of an alarm going off in the house. It was Monday morning, and normally, I'd be getting ready to meet Jameson at the shop, but today was anything but normal. It was the first day I'd have to go to work without AJ.

Heartache hit me like a tractor-trailer as I stretched and sat up. Jameson was gone; AJ was gone. I was alone. I wrapped the blanket around my naked body and looked out the front window. Jameson's car was still here, so where was he?

The shrill sound of the alarm was grating on my nerves. I ran upstairs to silence it and get in the shower. The hot water soothed my skin and the soreness I still felt from last night.

I finished my morning routine in a fog and headed back down the stairs. The keys were gone and there was a sticky note stuck to the hook by the door.

Went to work early, lots to do. I have the keys. See you soon. xo

All the lights were on in the shop as I walked down from the house. A loud shredding guitar blared through the open bay doors. Thick black smears snaked around Jameson's forearms, covering his hands and shirt. My heart skipped a beat. Jameson, grease, and rock-n-roll—those three things combined stimulated me to no end.

He wiped his hands on a dirty red rag as he saw me approach, and a simple swipe of his fingertip killed the music and left us in deafening quiet. "Mornin', cutie."

"What time did you get here this morning?"

"About five or so. You were unconscious." A slow smile crept across his lips and my cheeks grew hot. I didn't just fall asleep last night, I passed out from exertion.

"Why so early?"

He leaned against the car he was working on and crossed his long legs at the ankles. Jesus, he was sexy. "Well, the way I see it is, if I get here really early in the morning, I can get started on the Corvette without any interruptions. Then I can work on the regular stuff during the day and still get to leave here at a decent time to meet you at the hospital."

His answer blew me away. Not only was he attempting to take the reins in AJ's absence, but he still wanted to be there for me. As much as I appreciated his efforts, I couldn't possibly allow him to do all that for us. AJ almost killed himself working here solo for the last year, and since Jameson's arrival, there was more work now than there was then. "Jameson . . ."

"Before you tell me whatever it is that's rolling around in that gorgeous head of yours, just stop. I want to do this. After the way I left shit with AJ, I owe him this much. It's important to me. Now, do what you need to do and go on up to the hospital. I can handle this." Another quick swipe of his phone and Iron Maiden wailed through the huge concrete space.

The case was closed on the matter.

Jameson

JILLIAN WORKED UNTIL around lunchtime, then I told her to go. I'd arranged for the Firebird to be towed here, and there was no way in hell I was allowing her to see it. The moment the flatbed pulled into the lot, I knew I'd made the right decision. AJ's car was pretty much a pile of blue rubble. Its left side was caved in so badly, the car appeared to be in the shape of the letter V, and the middle bar where the T-tops should have been had a sickening bow at the top of it. Both panels of glass were missing, as was the driver's side door. I assume that was how they got him out.

My stomach coiled with nausea when I saw the interior. Shattered glass was everywhere. The front seat was completely torn away, and dried blood splattered the cracked windshield. By the looks of it, AJ was friggin' lucky he was alive.

The urge to vomit rose up my esophagus and I swallowed it down. It was a damn good thing I'd made Jillian leave. I cleaned out anything personal and got to work removing salvageable parts from under the hood to set aside for later use should we need them. When I finished, I called the scrap yard to come take it away. The thing needed to be gone before Jillian came home.

It was weird working in the shop without AJ. Using his tools almost felt wrong, even if there were good intentions behind it. After everything that happened, I had to make sure the shop didn't falter. I owed them both that much.

I'd told her I came into work early for the Corvette but that was only half-true. The nagging guilt that AJ was lying in that bed because of me was gnawing at me, making it hard to sleep. It never would have happened if he didn't walk in on us, and it's all my fault. I'm a grown man with no self-control. Even worse, I'm still doing it. Every time she comes to me in the night, I know it's wrong but I try to justify it by telling myself that I'm doing it for her. The truth is the only time I feel at home is when I'm with her.

I WAS EXHAUSTED by the end of the day but I forced myself into the shower and out to the hospital, stopping first at the do-nut shop to buy coffees for Jillian and me. At the last minute, I grabbed Jill a turkey sub because if I knew her, she hadn't eaten anything all day.

Jillian greeted me with a small smile when I knocked on the

doorframe to AJ's room. I handed her the coffee and sandwich, then retreated back to my chair in the hall. A few seconds later, she appeared in the doorway. "This was sweet, thank you." She blew into the coffee and steam rose from the mouth of the cup.

"How's he doing today?"

She leaned against the wall and exhaled a deep breath. "Same." The corners of her mouth turned down, and she took a sip of her coffee. "You don't have to wait out here, you know. You can come in."

"I read online that he may be able to hear talking and commotion that goes on inside the room. I think my voice is probably the last one he wants to hear, unfortunately. But maybe this will help stimulate some activity." I handed her my phone, and she peered down at the screen.

"2112, AJ's favorite. He loves Rush. I can't believe you remembered this."

"Geddy Lee is not a voice easily forgotten, believe me."

She smiled, and it seemed genuine for the first time in days. I watched from the hall as she turned back into the room and placed the phone on the table next to AJ. The pseudo futuristic sounds of "Overture" started up then smoothly tumbled into "The Temples of Syrinx." "And the meek shall inherit the Earth," she chanted under her breath. She kept the sound low, I assumed not to offend anyone else in the hospital. This was only for AJ, after all.

Memories of us trying to play this album came flooding back. It was both awful and awesome at the same time. I came far enough into the room to lean against the woodwork around the doorframe. She looked back at me. Tears streamed down her face, but she was smiling. Did she remember too? "You tried to sing the lead because even at sixteen, AJ's and my voices were too deep." She put her hands up to her mouth to stifle a giggle. She did remember.

"Everything seemed so simple back then. Strange how long five years can be." She wasn't kidding. It was a lifetime ago. The person I was back then was a stranger to me now. My lips curled into a tight-lipped smile, and I nodded, not wanting to say too much. I stepped out of the room and reclaimed my seat in the hall.

Eventually, the album ended, and all was quiet again except for the slight sounds of beeps and hums. Jill came out and handed my phone back to me, then returned to the seat next to AJ. Two seconds later, the phone buzzed in my hand.

After all is said and done, I know AJ would appreciate everything you're doing for us.

She must have texted herself from my phone to get my number. I saved her number into my phone before responding. Those ten digits were like gold.

Well, that's up for debate.

Considering the lethal look on his face when he found Jill and me in bed together, I wasn't so sure.

Maybe we can convince him what happened that day was just a dream.

Was that what she wanted? For us to just fade away like a dream? The idea that AJ's recovery equaled the possibility of never touching Jillian again created complicated feelings within me. Of course, I wanted him to be get better. I wanted nothing more than to make shit right between us. It was important to me that we have the man-to-man talk that was well overdue. Things got way out of hand before the accident, and I never should have let it get that far. I should have been straight with him from the start. I honestly had no idea what was going to happen once he recovered, but I did know I couldn't lose her. I needed her. She was a part of me now.

Maybe. I think being honest about our feelings would be a better tactic.

My knee bounced as I waited with my phone in my hand. Her response wasn't as immediate as her last, and I wondered if I'd overstepped my boundaries. I knew she was battling with it in her own mind. She mostly avoided me like the plague during the day, but at night, her true desires bubbled over.

Sex is not a feeling.

The text hit me in the chest like a sledgehammer. It was amazing how easily destroyed I was by those five little words. She was still denying us. When was she going to realize my feelings for her were real? I told her I wasn't going anywhere, and I meant it. Not just right now, but for always. If it took me the rest of my life to prove it to that girl, then I'd spend the rest of my life doing just that.

I slid my phone back into my pocket. There was no good way to respond. It was better to leave it alone before starting a wicked fight I knew I'd ultimately lose. She could tell herself that sex wasn't a feeling, but that night when she was pleading to have me inside her, I'd know the real deal.

CHAPTER NINETEEN

Jillian

THE NEXT TWO weeks progressed with little change except for the dark hair covering AJ's jaw. We'd fallen into this monotonous daily routine. Jameson worked like a machine at the shop, and I worked for a few hours, but ultimately left early to be with AJ, and every day I'd play different albums in AJ's room hoping he would hear it and follow it home.

I sat by AJ's bed waiting for Dr. Rumson to arrive. He'd had a CT scan earlier that morning, and I'd prayed for something to change. When she arrived, Jameson followed her in, and grabbed my hand, bracing me for the possibility of bad news.

She opened her folder and read the results from the chart before speaking. "Well, it seems like the swelling has greatly reduced." She pushed her glasses up on her nose and continued reading. "Brain activity seems normal as well." She closed the folder and held it under her arm.

I was squeezing Jameson's hand so hard it was beginning to hurt. "So what now?"

"Now, we lower the medicine and allow him to wake up." She said it so flatly; as if it wasn't the best news I've heard in my entire life. Jameson let go of my hand and wrapped his arms around me. I was so overwhelmed with emotions that I didn't know whether to cry or bang out a cartwheel. "Keep in mind it could take a while for the drugs to leave his system and even longer before we can remove the ventilator. Once he is stable, can open his eyes, can follow commands, and has shown strength to breathe by himself, there should be no reason that he can't be taken off the ventilator after a day or so, generally speaking."

"I understand. So when will you decrease the meds and when will he start to wake up?" I felt like a kid at Christmastime waiting to open her brand new bike. I was going to talk to my brother again. He was going to move and eventually talk back.

"We'll start decreasing them ASAP, but it could be tomorrow before we see any activity from him."

"Thank you so much, Dr. Rumson." If I didn't think the woman would suffer cardiac arrest from the shock, I probably would have kissed her. She checked the machines, tinkered with the IV bags, and excused herself. I sat back in the seat by AJ, content to wait until he was ready to join me again. Jameson kissed my head and walked back to his chosen seat in the hallway.

I scrolled through my phone looking for another album to play. It felt like a Van Halen kind of day. I popped on *1984,* and set it on his bedside table as I'd done every day that week. Diamond Dave started to croon, and I joined Jameson in the hall. "You all right? You seem weird."

"Yeah, cutie, I'm great. Just tired. It's been a long couple of weeks, you know?" I hadn't noticed how worn out he really looked until he said something. He'd been burning the candle at both ends between the shop and dealing with all of this.

"Why don't you head out? I'm fine here, really."

"Nah, I'm good." He threaded his fingers with mine and pulled me between his legs. His arms encircled my middle and squeezed me tightly. "See? I'm better already."

I smiled and took a step back. He seemed so odd. His eyes were ringed red with exhaustion, but it was more than that. The sadness in them was painful to look at.

"Jameson, you've been amazing this week," I said resting my hands along each stubbly cheek. "You've done more for us than anyone ever has, and there is no way I could possibly ever repay you. Please, go home and get some rest. For me."

He looked up at me with a bleak expression. It was almost as if he was afraid to leave. Like if he left this spot, I'd dissolve into a puddle of nothingness on the floor never to be seen again. "You and I both know I'm not above begging," I said with a smirk. "Honestly, I'm probably just going to stay the night. I would like to be here when he wakes up, ya know?"

"All right, all right. You win." He stood, stretching his long body to the ceiling. The corded muscles in his arms flexed and strained under his vibrant skin and his rigid stomach peeked out from the hem of his shirt. I pretended not to notice the hard looks he got from the women on the floor.

His fingers caught under my chin as his lips dropped to mine with a gentle kiss good-bye that took my breath away. "Call me if you need anything," he said, before walking toward the elevator.

"Hot for Teacher" was just starting to play as I reentered AJ's room. Alex Van Halen thrashed on the drums and the eyes beneath AJ's closed lids started to flit side to side. My mouth dropped open in surprise; this was more activity than I've seen from him all week! Small as it was, it gave me more hope than the doctor's encouraging words did earlier. My mind was made up. I would not leave this hospital until AJ opened his eyes.

AJ's favorite bands played one after the other late into the night, but I didn't get any other indication that he was with me at all. I was doing the bobble head neck bounce trying to keep myself from nodding off in the chair. My eyelids felt heavy, but

I just knew the second my eyes closed, his would open and I'd miss it.

I rubbed my eyes and got up to get another coffee. Jameson's unoccupied seat sent a quick flash of sadness through me. I sent him home because he needed rest, but I wished he were still here. I couldn't help it. It was lonely here at night, and I missed him. I wished I were home in his arms. He was so cozy and warm. He'd tangle his legs with mine and wrap his arm completely around me in a sweet Jameson cocoon. His warm breath would tickle my neck and the loneliness would drift away leaving me with a sense of peace.

Every night this week, we'd started the night out apart but finished it together. He'd tuck me in and do whatever needed to be done at the house, but sooner or later, when the nightmares hit, I'd crawl into his arms and he'd comfort me the best way he knew how. It was the part of our routine that was ignored the moment the sun rose.

I grabbed a coffee from the machine in the ICU waiting room. Unlike the stuff in the coffee shop downstairs, it was total swill, but I hoped enough cream and sugar would mask the taste. This time of night, it was all that was available, and I needed the jolt of caffeine to stay awake.

The music stopped and the room was quiet. I sipped my coffee and sat in silence until I couldn't take it anymore. "Remember that time in high school when we went to Ozzfest together? That was a wild show. Our seats were right at the edge of the wall in the stadium. It would only be one swift jump to the ground for us to be on the floor. You talked about it the whole time we were there, but I was too chicken to make the leap." My throat felt tight conjuring up the memory of a lifetime ago. AJ and I were different then, wild and carefree. We had nothing better to do than hang out.

"Pantera came on stage, and you lost your mind. The

growling vocals of Phil Anselmo made me feel brave, and I went for it. I jumped over the wall and landed on the floor below. You followed me right after yelling, 'Go! Go!' so that we could get lost in the crowd. It was exhilarating, and I wished I hadn't been so scared and listened to you earlier. I should have known you'd never ask me to do something that would get me hurt. You always have my back."

Tears filled my eyes. I wiped them away and cleared my throat before continuing with my anecdote. "That was, of course, until I ran into the mosh pit!" I giggled as the full memory of that day came flooding back. "I took a rogue elbow to the face and some enormous beefy dude grabbed the kid by his shirt and hurled him aside like he was a kitten, remember? I think that is one of my favorite memories of us. I ended up with a bloody nose and the worst sunburn of my life, but that show was legendary. And I got to see it with my favorite person in the whole world."

As I finished my story, I slid my hand into the motionless one lying by his side. His fingers lightly squeezed around mine then let go. I jumped up from my seat. "AJ?" My voice was quiet, but my heart was pounding in my chest. I gave another tentative squeeze, and his hand tightened around mine again. My hand still in his, I touched his face with the other. "AJ. It's Jill. Can you hear me?"

His lashes flickered, and his hand constricted again, but his eyes didn't open. I stroked his cheek with my thumb and waited. I knew I should probably get a nurse, but I was glued to the spot next to his bed. "AJ, I know you can hear me. Please, come back."

Nothing happened. Disappointed tears flooded out of both eyes. How much longer could I do this for? I was trying so hard to be strong, but every time I got an inkling of progress, it disappeared without any warning and crushed me.

It just wasn't fair. Why did everything have to be so damned hard all the time? I felt like I'd been put on this Earth for someone's sick amusement. Like, 'let's see how much shit the short girl can take before she completely breaks!' Well, I hope whoever was watching because my breaking point was very near.

Dead tired and angry at the world, my ass hit the chair as my pity party continued. All I wanted was for AJ to open his damn eyes. It seemed like such a small request after everything else I'd been through in my short lifetime. Why was I being punished like this? What kind of bastard was I in a past life that I was destined to live through watching everyone I love rot away in front of my very eyes while I was powerless to stop it?

What I really needed was sleep. I'd been running on fumes, and I was starting to lose my shit. Covering my face with a tissue, I wiped all the wetness away and took a few deep breaths. The doctor said he would wake up, and I had to be patient. Falling apart wasn't going to help matters. I sighed heavily and laid my head on the bed next to my brother.

Fingers touched my face, and I shot up. AJ's eyelids fluttered and blinked and his eyes slowly began to open. I grasped his hand and pushed the call button to alert the nurse as I awaited my brother to come to.

His eyes looked drugged. I wasn't sure if he would even know what was happening. "AJ, I'm here. I'm here." Lethargic pupils moved at a snail's pace in my direction. "You're awake."

I couldn't contain the tears that spilled over my cheeks. His drowsy lids closed and opened again, and it seemed like he tried to say something. "Don't talk. It's okay. You're in a hospital. You had an accident. You're going to be fine, though. Everything is going to be fine." I was assuring myself just as much as him. He wasn't out of the dark yet, but seeing his hazel eyes staring back at me was the greatest sight in the world to me.

Jameson

THE SHRILL RINGING of the phone next to my head woke me up. The lighted display illuminated the dark room. I was still half-asleep when I barked hello into the mouthpiece.

"It's eight o'clock, are you still in bed?" Her sweet voice flowed into my ear like a song.

"Shit, yeah. I had trouble sleeping last night." It had only been a couple of weeks, but I'd grown used to having her next to me. My cold bed was like a prison cot without her sweet smell and soft body next to mine. It made even their lumpy old couch feel comfortable. "You okay? How's AJ?"

"I'm great. AJ woke up early this morning. He was still pretty drugged up and doesn't seem all that with it," she said with a sleepy yawn leaking into her sentence.

"That's great! Have you been awake all night?"

"I slept a little in the chair in the room. Catnaps mostly. AJ is asleep again, on his own this time. They are going to be doing some more tests on him, so I'm going to head home in a bit to sleep and shower. I just wanted to give you an update."

"All right, cutie. You be safe driving home." I disconnected the call and jumped out of bed to get ready to open the shop. If I didn't hustle, I was going to be late, and I wanted to stop at the grocery store to get some things for Jill before heading over. I wasn't sure when she'd be back, but I did know that if there was no food when she got there, she just wouldn't eat. She couldn't survive on coffee and catnaps alone.

The key to her house was on the key ring for the office, so I just let myself in the front door when I arrived. I filled her fridge with a couple of sandwiches and a bottle of that Hazelnut shit she liked to pour in her coffee. It wasn't much, but it would suffice for now.

The sound of crunching gravel outside alerted me to her presence. It was ridiculous how excited I was to see her. It had only been one night, but I missed her. The front door opened, and I walked over to meet her. "Honey, you're home!" I joked.

She seemed surprised to see me. "What are you doing here?"

"I was just about to go open the shop. I stopped here first to put some stuff in the fridge for you."

Her sleepy face split into a wicked grin. "What's so funny?" I asked.

"You're kind of like my bitch." She laughed. I stuck my lip out in a playful pout as if I was offended by her taunting. Truth was she was right. There wasn't a thing I wouldn't do for her. I was most definitely her bitch.

"Get some sleep, cutie. I'll see ya later," I said, dropping a kiss to her head and letting myself out the door to start another grueling day at the office.

CHAPTER TWENTY

Jillian

AJ'S IMPROVEMENT WAS gradual but constant. Once the vent tube was removed, he started to seem like his old self again.

Jameson never returned to the hospital. In fact, I barely saw much of him at all in the weeks since AJ became lucid. He still went to the shop every day, but things between us were different. He'd cared for me so lovingly those first few weeks, and I felt so lucky to have him in my life. AJ was on the road to recovery, though, and I had to make a choice. My brother had to come first.

"You don't have to sit here with me every day, sis. I'm going to survive, I promise." AJ's shoulder was still in a sling, but the gash on his head was healing. It wouldn't be long until he was coming home.

"Whatever. You just don't want me to see you hitting on the hot nurses." His grin made my heart smile. I'd admit my constant presence at the hospital was probably a little annoying, but I'd come so close to losing him. I wasn't ready to retract my clingy claws yet. "Don't worry, I'm checking in at the shop and getting stuff done there. I haven't let everything fall to hell."

"He's still showing up?" The light in his eyes went dim at

the mention of Jameson. Naturally, when he'd asked about the shop, I told him Jameson was picking up the slack.

"Yeah, he is. I told you, he's handling pretty much everything down there. He's been amazing."

A sneer flashed on his lips then disappeared. "Yeah, I'm sure he has."

"What's that supposed to mean?" Every time the topic of conversation turned to Jameson, I could see the hostility in AJ returning. "I really don't get you, you know that? You should be happy you have a friend like him. He doesn't have to be down there busting his ass, doing the work of two men, but he is."

"Jameson's not my friend, he's my employee." The sneer returned to his face. After everything he'd been through, I couldn't believe he was still angry.

"You're acting like a pissed off toddler with a broken toy. It happened, AJ." I didn't have to say out loud what "it" meant. The look on his face told me he understood. "Get over it."

His lips pursed, and his eyes turned to slits. "It's late and I'm tired. Go home, Jillian." I could feel the anger building in my gut. I took Jameson's side, and he completely shut down. The battle between my head and my heart continued to rage inside me as I walked to my truck. AJ was such a stubborn ass. If only he was able to see Jameson through my eyes. He'd see a man who'd stop at nothing to make sure I was protected and cared for. He'd see a man just like himself.

Jameson's car was still parked in front of the shop. The pangs of guilt reared their ugly heads. I'd been avoiding him like the plague, and he was still working into the night making sure my family's business thrived. More than anything, I wanted to run into that shop and cover him in kisses. I wanted to not only tell him how thankful I was for his presence in my life, but I also wanted to show him. The more I thought about it, the more overwhelming and painful the desire became. But I couldn't do any of those things. AJ would never allow it, and I needed my brother's blessing.

The truck rolled past the shop, and my phone chimed as I made my way up the steps of my house.

Gonna drive right by without a word, huh?

Jameson's text caught me off guard. We'd had the occasional text chat here and there, mostly about the shop or AJ.

Sorry, in a rush is all.

I hadn't gotten past my front door when I heard the chime again.

I miss you, cutie. How long do you intend to leave me hanging here?

My brain clouded over. I didn't want his words to hang in the air unanswered, but I couldn't come up with anything to send in response. It wasn't up to me to decide. I'd missed my window of opportunity and my phone chimed again.

I'm waiting . . .

He had me flustered. He was trying to get a rise out of me, and it was working. I didn't want him to have this kind of effect on me. I wanted to go back to when everything was simple and easy. When I didn't wake up thinking about his smile and go to bed smelling him on my sheets. It had been weeks since he touched me, but I could still feel his hands all over my skin and I ached to have him hold me. He was killing me slowly with every pleading message he sent. I jammed my phone into my pocket. This conversation was over.

"Jillian." My name blew through the air as if being carried by the wind. I turned, and Jameson was there. The heat in his eyes worked its way into my soul attempting to melt my hesitation to run to him. His hand fidgeted at his side, and the other fisted his phone in a vise grip. My pulse raced as he pinned me to the porch with his gaze. "I'm trying to be a good guy, cutie. I'm trying to give you the space you need, but I don't deserve this cold shoulder."

"What do you want from me?" My voice trembled from his admission. He was a good guy, and I'd been awful to him. He continued to give me all of him, and all I did in return was take.

"I want you to tell me the truth. Do you still want me or not?"

Well, there it was. The answer was an emphatic yes. I didn't just want him, I craved him. He was the air in my lungs and the water on my tongue, my soft bed and my hot shower. He was everything I desired, except for the one thing I needed most: my brother's approval. "He'll never accept it, Jameson."

He stalked closer to where I stood on the porch. "That wasn't my question."

"I don't have another answer to give you." I closed my eyes and turned my back to him. The front door opened, and the darkness of the empty house sucked me inside.

Jameson

I LAY ON my bed with my heart in pieces. I handed it to her on a silver platter, and she crushed it in her tiny hands. The woman was infuriating. She drove me crazy on so many levels it boggled my mind. If I were smart, I'd throw in the towel on all of this while I still had an ounce of dignity left, but the thought of not being with her caused my chest to burn.

Leaving town wasn't an option, but leaving this room was necessary. These four walls threatened to close in on me if I stayed here any longer. I grabbed my keys and locked the door behind me.

I had no idea where I was going, so I just drove. Memories of her were everywhere around me. She was never mine to begin with. I'd had her for a brief moment, but it was an illusion.

I turned the wheel and cursed myself for being such a pussy. Against my better judgment, I allowed Jillian to get under my skin, and now, I'll never get her out. She'll live there forever, crushing me from the inside. Coming back to this stupid town was a mistake. There'd never been anything here for me except heartache.

My past was bogging me down. I should have been up front from the start, but it was too late to go back and undo what I'd done wrong. I could only move forward and make things right.

My phone began to vibrate in my pocket, and I pulled the car over to fish it out.

Come over

There was no explanation, just two little words. A demand. I cursed at myself again as I threw my phone on the passenger seat and turned the car around.

The area around her house was dark, except for the yellow glow of her porch light. I made the short journey from my car to her steps, and the door flew open as if she'd been waiting for me. Her lips were on mine in an instant. Her mouth was tangy and sweet like limes and something else.

Tequila?

Her hands fisted my hair. She climbed me like a spider monkey before I even made it completely inside. The sole of my boot smacked against the door, slamming it shut before I carried her to the couch.

Her clumsy hands fumbled with the button on my pants, and I grabbed them. "Wait." I tried to catch her gaze, but her eyes were unfocused. The smell of booze wafted off her with each panting breath. She was hammered. "What are you doing, Jill? What is this?"

"Giving you an answer. You asked if I want you, my answer is yes."

She lunged toward me to kiss me again, and I pulled my head away. "Do you want *me*? Or do you just want my dick?"

She shook her head confused. "Does it make a difference?"

"Yes, it makes a difference!" I jumped off the couch to keep her from touching me again. My head and my cock were about to fight to the death, and I needed to be less close to her. "I want more than this, Jillian. I want *you*. All of you."

"But I'm giving you all of me. Come take it." She lifted her arms out to the side as if sacrificing herself to me. Her pleading eyes pulled me back down to the couch next to her.

"You don't get it," I said gently. "It's not enough for me." I put my hand high up on her thigh, my thumb resting mere centimeters from her center. "I don't just want to be here." My hand left her leg and covered her heart. "I want to be here."

Her eyes dropped to my hand then back up at me. She pulled her bottom lip between her teeth, and my hand touched her face. "I don't want to hide anymore. It's not enough to just be your secret fuck buddy. I want to be yours completely."

"I would love that." Her voice was barely a whisper.

"Then stop fighting this." My hands came up on either side of her face so she couldn't look away. She needed to face the truth. We belonged together.

Her eyes welled with tears. "I can't."

Dropping my hands, I stood. The testosterone coursed through my bloodstream, and I needed to lash out. "Why, Jillian? Tell me why and don't fucking tell me it's because of AJ."

"What do you want me to say, Jameson?" She jumped off the couch and circled the room as she continued. "You know how AJ feels about us. What am I supposed to do? Alienate my only relative, my best friend, and my business partner all in one fell swoop?" She stopped in front of me and crossed her arms. "And when all of that is said and done, tell me. What do I do then, when shit gets too real and you vanish into thin air?"

She might as well have stabbed me with a kitchen knife. My mouth dropped open as I stared down at her in disbelief. I took a deep breath and blew it out hard, glaring down at her before I found the words to respond to her vicious remark.

"Have I given you any indication that I'm leaving?" I took a step closer to her. She wavered from the alcohol but stood her ground. Her breathing accelerated and her lips parted. "You've raked me over hot coals. You've used me and thrown me away at your will, and I keep coming back for more. What else do I have to do to prove to you that I'm not going anywhere?"

She swallowed hard. "When I think of something, I'll let you know." Her voice quivered, but her fiery eyes held my gaze. This girl was going to be the death of me.

"Good, you do that." I backed off and headed toward the door. My blood was pumping through my body at a feverish pace. I was tempted to throw her to the floor and take my aggression out on her until the sun came up, but that shit would only complicate things.

"What was her name?"

The question stopped me cold. I stood at the edge of the room and stared down at the frayed edge of the area rug. "Marie." My voice hitched under the knot in my throat. I hadn't spoken her name out loud in years. After all this time, I still felt a bitter sting as it rolled off my tongue. I can see her face, cold and calculating, as she unloaded the heinous admission that led me to run.

"Why did you leave them?" she asked, calmly. There wasn't malice or pity behind the question.

I looked over my shoulder and saw her standing in the same spot I'd left her. The fire in her eyes had fizzled out and was replaced with empathy. I rubbed a hand down my face and sighed. "They were never mine to begin with."

CHAPTER TWENTY-ONE

Jillian

THE BLINDING SUN filtered in through my bedroom window. I winced in pain, cursing my headache and wishing I hadn't drank so much the night before. After my confrontation with Jameson, I was too wound up to sleep. Drinking my weight in tequila was not the smartest idea. My mouth tasted like death. I needed water and aspirin, stat.

I forced myself up and into the bathroom. As much as I wanted to stay in bed and sleep, I had to go into the shop to do some billing, and Jameson needed to be paid. Texting him for a booty call was not my finest hour. The thought of facing him made me want to hurl. Actually, I kind of wanted to hurl anyway, thanks to the alcohol.

My eyes raked over the contents of the medicine cabinet in search of something to ease my throbbing head. Band-Aids, Q-tips, mouthwash, tampons . . .

The half-full box of tampons held my attention. When was my last period? Dates on the calendar ran through my cloudy brain. I'd never kept track before. I never had a reason to. Until recently.

I racked my brain trying to formulate a way to narrow it down. Was it hot out or just warm? Did I have it before our trip to the shore? After? I was positive I'd skipped July completely. I'd been so overwhelmed I just couldn't remember.

My head was in the toilet in an instant. All the alcohol wretched out like a fire hose until I was empty. I sat on the cold tile with my head resting on the seat of the toilet. We'd been careful. I mentally recalled each and every time we'd been together and he always wore a condom. Every time. Except that one time . . .

The memory of us on the couch invaded my brain. My impatience. I was hurting and needed him to ease the pain. I pulled him in and we never stopped to think about the consequences.

The dull ache in my head became a steady pound. How could I have let this happen? After everything I'd learned about Jameson and that girl, I went and did the same thing. I allowed myself to be controlled by my impulses and flushed my life, much like my vomit, down the toilet.

I couldn't control the shaking from deep inside my gut. A hundred thoughts raced through my brain but one in particular jumped out from all of them like a geyser. If I tell Jameson, he's going to leave. He was single handedly running the shop while AJ was recovering, and we needed him now more than ever. Life had handed me a giant shit sandwich, but the only person I had to blame for the taste in my mouth now was me.

There was no way I was going to get through the day until I knew for sure. My feet propelled me into the shower. Without bothering to dry my hair, I ran out of the house forgetting to lock the door behind me.

I stood in the Family Planning aisle at the store feeling like a statistic. The pregnancy test options were endless. Blue strips, pink strips—the whole aisle seemed to be spinning. I grabbed one and ran up to the checkout to complete the purchase that could potentially seal my fate forever.

I pulled into the shop, unlocked the door, and made a

beeline for the bathroom. With trembling fingers, I tore open the box but dropped everything on the floor and the plastic strip clattered along the tile. I snatched it from the floor and held it under the stream of urine, counting to ten like the directions said.

The test balanced on the edge of the sink as I waited for the results. My heart thrummed against my ribcage so hard it felt bruised. *Two lines pregnant, one line not.* I said it over and over in my mind as I chewed my thumbnail almost bloody.

A knock on the door caused me to jump out of my skin. "Are you all right?" Even after I'd been so hurtful to him yesterday, he was still concerned about my welfare. He belonged in this bathroom with me, holding my hand while we waited together. He told me I'd never be alone, but here I was scared to death, while he got the satisfaction of never knowing the fear that I was feeling at this very moment.

"Yeah, I'll be right out." With rattled nerves, I took a deep breath and lifted the strip off the sink. The answer I desired was clearly defined behind the tiny plastic window. I looked up at the ceiling and exhaled slowly. My shoulders dropped from their position at my ears. I waited until the hammering of my heart subsided then stashed the evidence.

I dodged a bullet. Now, I had to open the door and face the smoking gun that waited for me on the other side.

Jameson

THE OFFICE WAS unlocked, but Jillian wasn't inside. A thin slice of light highlighted the tile under the bathroom door. I turned on the lights and opened the bay doors in the shop, and she never came out.

She's probably sick as hell from last night.

I knocked lightly on the door. "Are you all right?"

Her voice was strained as it came through the door. "Yeah, I'll be right out."

A few minutes later, the door opened. She looked like hell. "Are you sure you're okay?"

"Yeah, I'll survive. Pretty sure I just drank too much last night."

My brows creased together at the sight of her pale skin and glassy eyes. I had no doubts she was hung over, but there was something more she wasn't telling me. "Well, let me know if you need anything."

I began to head into the shop to get to work but her fingers closed around my bicep. "If the baby wasn't yours, who's was it?"

"That's a conversation for another time, cutie." It was a conversation I never intended to have period. I was eventually going to have to tell her everything, but I didn't have the energy for it now. She dropped her hand, and I went to work.

Old feelings came flooding back as I rummaged around the tool bench chucking things out of my way. Mine was a disturbing situation I couldn't even begin to wrap my brain around. There wasn't a day that goes by that I didn't regret my decision, but I was just so angry. I was a stupid kid, and I believed all her lies.

I thought of my father and his bullshit speech about responsibilities. What a joke. The chip on my shoulder started to weigh me down the more I thought of him and his smug face when I told him Marie was pregnant. He put his arm around me and told me he'd support me. I promised I'd take care of her, but I couldn't even be in the same room as her anymore after I found out the truth.

My anger was spiraling like a tornado, intent on destroying everything in its path. My work was sloppy. I jammed a screwdriver between the cylinder and the back plate to pop the gasket off a brake drum. The screwdriver slipped and stabbed into the meaty part of my hand. I cursed and the tool in my hand clattered onto the ground.

The shop did not have anything to sop up the blood that started collecting in my palm. I closed my fist and ran into the office. Jillian was on the phone. Blood trailed down my forearm leaving a row of tiny red drops from the door of the office to the bathroom. I kicked the door closed and ran cold water over my aching hand as I began to wash the cut out in the sink.

"Jameson? There's blood everywhere. What the hell happened?" The knob on the bathroom door rattled as she opened it.

"I cut myself in the shop. It's pretty bad, you don't wanna see it."

"Don't be a baby, give it here." She lifted my hand out of the sink and looked. The skin on my palm was torn wide open. Blood seeped out from the dark red gash in the center. "Yeah, you got yourself good. You're going to need a hospital. Let me grab the first-aid kit from the house to bandage this up."

She ran out the door while I wadded toilet paper in my fist and sat on the lid of the toilet, hoping like hell the bleeding stopped on its own and I didn't need stitches. Blood soaked the paper as I watched it turn from white to red before my very eyes. I chucked the wad in the trash bin and grabbed another one. A square of paper caught my eye as I looked around the floor to make sure I hadn't left any drops of red on the light tile. It was lying on the floor face up between the trashcan and the toilet where I sat. A drug store receipt with that day's date.

I slid the paper along the ground with my foot until I was able to comfortably bend down to pick it up. The pain in my hand became a memory as I read the contents of the receipt. Goose bumps broke out on my skin.

Hungover my ass.

Jillian was pregnant.

My arm dropped to my lap and the receipt drifted to the floor. My hands were shaking. The tiny bathroom felt claustrophobic.

I was going to be a dad.

I had a little money put away, but it wasn't enough to start a family with. The only thing I owned that had any value at all was my car, and the backseat didn't even have seat belts. I didn't even know if I'd still have a job when AJ returned to the shop, but I knew one thing for sure. If I had to work like a dog for the rest of my life to ensure Jillian and our kid had the best lives possible, then that was what I intended to do.

A thought wrapped its hands around my throat and squeezed. She didn't tell me. I stood on the other side of the door while she was in here alone. Dampness filled my eyes. I wondered if she planned to tell me at all.

She doesn't trust me.

I had to find some way to prove to her that I was in this for life. We would raise the baby together. That girl was everything to me, and our kid would be too.

The front door buzzed, and I swiped the receipt off the floor and shoved it into my pocket. Confronting her about it now would only be a waste of time. I knew what I had to do.

"How's it looking?" A tiny white box marked with a red cross on the front dangled from her fingertips as she held out her hand to take a look at my wound. She appeared different to me now. She was always beautiful, but there was something about knowing she was growing a piece of me inside her that took my breath away. We were in no way ready for this, but when I looked at her, any residual fear I had about the future vanished. Jillian was my future.

"It's bleeding pretty badly still." I held up the blood soaked toilet paper wad in my hand and she scrunched her nose.

She lifted the wad with her thumb and forefinger and dropped it into the trash with the other one. She padded the wound with a thick layer of gauze and wrapped it with an ace bandage. "Let's go, I'll drive."

"No, we can't leave the shop unattended. I'll go, don't worry about it." I stood to leave but she stopped me.

"Jameson, you can't drive with your hand like that!"

"It's my left hand, I'll be fine."

"Oh, yeah? How are you going to steer and work the stick shift, brainiac?" She blinked her long lashes at me as if she'd backed me into a corner.

"My hands are magic, baby. I can do things you can't even begin to imagine." I waggled my brows at her and the corner of her mouth turned up.

"You're a dork. Okay, have at it. Good luck." She moved to the side and let me by.

"Thanks." Our bodies touched as I passed through the door and my good hand absentmindedly grazed her stomach. I got in my car and drove to Crestmere Hospital.

It was time AJ knew the truth.

CHAPTER 22

Jameson

MY KNEE BOUNCED up and down as the doctor stitched me up, but it wasn't because of my hand. As soon as I was finished, I was going to head up and see AJ. The timing was terrible, but I didn't have the luxury of waiting for the right moment. We needed to get our shit squared away now.

I left the E.R. with a brand new bandage and a nervous stomach as I punched the button on the elevator to go up to his room. It was ridiculous how nervous I was. I felt like I was meeting the girl's father for the first time. This was AJ. He was my best friend and the most logical guy I knew. I was just going to walk in there and lay it all on the line for him.

I took a deep breath as I walked off the elevator. It was now or never. A couple nurses recognized me and waved as I passed, but I kept moving toward the door. It was open and he was sitting in Jillian's chair watching television.

I knocked on the door frame. "Hey man, how's it going?"

He turned and saw me, then stared straight ahead at the television again. "Jameson." His tone was cold. He was definitely not happy to see me.

I walked in anyway, intent to have the conversation I went there to have. "Glad to see you up and about, man. You scared us there for a while." I leaned against the wall in front of him hoping to melt his icy facade.

"Us?"

"Yeah, Jillian and me."

He snorted out a nasty noise when I lumped her name in with mine. Jillian and I were destined to be an "us." He better get used to it.

"Listen dude, we gotta talk."

His lids narrowed and his eyes rolled. "Pretty sure I said everything I needed to say."

"Yeah, well I didn't. You destroyed me that day, dude. There's so much you don't know, and it's time you heard the truth."

"Why should I give a shit about anything you have to say?"

"Because I'm in love with your sister. Hearing that probably pisses you off, but it's the truth." I tapped my fist on my chest to drive my point home. "I love her, man. You came in there and blew up my past without knowing the whole story and she rung me out to dry."

AJ sat there quiet for a moment. His eyes glared in my direction and I could see the wheels turning in his head. His face was unreadable. I wasn't sure if he was going to allow me to continue or tell me to go fuck myself. My heart was beating out of my chest as I waited for his response to my admission.

"You love her huh? All right lover boy, you have the floor. Tell me what it is you love so much about her." He leaned back in his chair and crossed an ankle over his knee. He was testing me. AJ was as stubborn as his sister.

I blew out an exasperated breath. *He wanted to see me grovel? Hell with it, I'll grovel.*

I thought about it for a minute before opening my mouth. There were so many things to love about her, how could I choose just one? "I love how her eyes sparkle when she's happy and how her tiny body can create such an enormous presence. She feels with her entire being. Her laugh is like music. Her heart is so full that sometimes I can see it boiling over."

Once I started, it all just tumbled out like dominoes. I pushed myself off the wall and paced the room as I bared my soul.

"I love how she can rock out hard as concrete, but still be soft as cotton. She doesn't need dresses or makeup or any of that other shit to be beautiful. She is gorgeous just the way she is. She's a wise ass, a pain in the ass and doesn't hesitate to kick ass."

I stopped pacing and stood in front of AJ. "I'm amazed by the way she loves you, dude. It's unconditional. She's wholesome and she's pure."

His eyes softened. My pacing continued as I started counting off more items on my fingers.

"She's smart, she's strong, she's funny, she's sexy. . . . ."

"All right all right. Stop, I get it." He put his hand up ending my rant and exhaled hard through his nose. "She know how you feel about her?"

"Sort of. But she won't give me the time of day because of you. Your approval means more to her than anything." I sat on the corner of the bed, my lips turned down at the edges. My knee continued to bounce, and I leaned forward on my elbows to stop it.

He rubbed his eye with his knuckle. I could see how tired he was, but this couldn't wait. "So, what do you want from me, dude? My blessing? You're just not good enough for her."

I pulled my lips into a thin line contemplating what he said. He was right. Jillian was better than me in every way imaginable. "I know, man. But I'm willing to spend the rest of my life trying to be."

His head moved up and down in a slow nod as he eyed me

warily, probably trying to see if I'm full of shit or not. "You got my attention. Tell me what you came here to say."

I stood up from my spot on the bed and walked over to the wall where I was standing earlier. I picked at the bandage on my hand then ran my fingers through my hair. Complicated emotions began to drown me as I brought myself back to the day when my entire life changed.

"Marie was pregnant, that part is the truth. The part you don't know is, she was already pregnant when we slept together."

CHAPTER 23

Jameson

BROKEN SHARDS OF the memory crashed down on me like glass. Each time I thought about it, a new wound opened until I was stripped bare of my skin lying vulnerable to the elements.

I met her in the mall. She approached me loitering in front of Jamba Juice without a care in the world. You could see in her face she was about my age, but that was where the similarities stopped. She was tall with bleached hair and the tiniest skirt I'd ever seen. "You wanna buy me a smoothie, handsome?"

White blond hair twirled around her fingers as she smiled at me. I was young, but this wasn't my first trip to the rodeo. By the time I was sixteen, I was already bigger than most of the guys in my class and the girls had started to respond.

She sat in the food court, sipping her Banana Berry smoothie giggling at my stupid jokes. I poured on the charm, hoping like hell she would let me kiss her. In hindsight, I shouldn't have bothered trying so hard. Marie was a sure thing.

By the time we hit the bus, her fingers were already inching up my thigh. Once inside, her hands roamed my chest then slipped down my pants before we'd even turned on the television. I'd banged a few girls already by that point, but Marie was different. They were usually demure and just laid there. She came at me like it was her job. This girl was aggressive, and it was hot.

When my dad got home, she was still there. "Hi, Mr. Tate. It's nice to meet you." Her voice purred like a kitten as she held her hand out for my father to shake. The look on his face was one I'd never seen before. It eluded me at the time, but now I know it was a mixture of fear and guilt.

A few weeks later, she showed up on my doorstep. A duffel bag was slung over her shoulder and her face was emotionless. "I'm pregnant." She blurted it out like she was talking about the weather. As if it was no big deal that my life had come to an abrupt halt.

There had to be some mistake. We'd only slept together once, but she claimed I was her first. She held up the grainy photo and I saw it: a tiny white bean in a sea of blackness. The beginnings of a life inside the cavern of her body. A life I put there.

"She's your responsibility now, son. You gotta take care of it." My dad was so calm when I told him. His teenage son had knocked up some random chick he met at the mall, and he wasn't even angry about it. "She'll stay here and you'll be a man."

Thoughts swam through my head as I made a plan for the new future ahead of me. A future that included a girl I didn't want and a baby I wasn't prepared for. I would quit school, get a job, leave the band and all that childish shit behind me. Eventually, I would marry her. It was the right thing to do.

I called AJ and asked if he thought his dad would hire me. He sat silent on the other end as I told him about Marie and the trouble I'd gotten myself into. "It's gonna work out, bro. We'll sit down with my dad and figure it out." That was the last conversation AJ and I had until I showed up at the shop five years later.

Marie settled into our house easily, she in my bed and me on the couch. She, much like my father, didn't seem to give a rat's ass about my presence. Our relationship wasn't romantic. When I looked at her a second time, the initial excitement was gone. I didn't even think she *was that pretty. The only thing I felt for her now was regret.*

I woke in the night, stumbling to the bathroom in the dark, the urge to pee outweighing my need for sleep. The light shining from the cracked open door of my dad's room caught my eye. " . . . come on, baby, don't be mad . . ."

Marie's raspy voice came through the door. I walked closer, confused about why she was in his room in the first place.

"You fucked my son. What would possess you to do such a thing?"

"I was desperate, baby. But look; now, we can all be together." I peeked in through the crack and saw them in the room. My father was sitting on the edge of his bed, and Marie was walking toward him. She lifted his hand with hers, put his finger in her mouth down to the knuckle, then drew it out and licked her lips. "That cheap imitation was nothing like the real thing."

My heart jackhammered in my chest. What the hell was going on? Marie and my dad?

He yanked his hand out of her grasp. "You're a crazy bitch, you know that?"

Her face twisted into a pissed off knot and her hands landed protectively over her stomach. "I'm the crazy bitch carrying your kid. Whether he calls you Daddy or Grandpa doesn't make a difference to me, but my ass is here to stay. Get used to it."

My hands shook at my side. My vision blurred with a rage I'd never felt before. If I had gone into that room, I would be telling this story from a jail cell serving life in prison for murder. My own father was going to allow me to destroy my life cleaning up a mess he'd made with a girl who was younger than I was.

All the tumblers fell into place. Marie didn't randomly see me in the mall, she sought me out. My father had cast her aside, so she latched onto me knowing it would put her back into his life. She really was a crazy bitch.

My mind was so full of fury that I wasn't thinking straight. The violent thoughts in my head were terrifying me beyond belief. Visions of wrapping my hands around his windpipe played through my mind on a loop. He should be the one dead, not my mother.

If I didn't get away from this situation, I'd only make matters worse and do something I couldn't undo. Backing away from the door, numb with shock and resentment, I grabbed a change of clothes, my wallet, and my bank book. I walked to the bus station and got on the very first bus. I didn't care where it was going; all I knew at that moment was that I was never coming back.

"A few days later, I was calm enough to call home. I needed to hear it myself from the bastard's mouth. Instead, my father told me Marie killed herself and that it was all my fault. He said he never wanted to see me again and that was fine with me. He'd never wanted me anyway."

I finished my story and waited for AJ to say something. The blood had drained from his face, and he sat there staring at me in disbelief.

"My father was a bad man. The things he did were so vile and disturbing that I never wanted anyone to know about them. I would rather be remembered as a loser who ran out on his pregnant girlfriend than the son of a fucking pedophile." Averting my gaze, I wiped my cheek with the back of my hand embarrassed about the wetness on my face

"Damn, man," AJ said after a while. "So why *did* you come back?"

"My mom had set up a trust fund for me when I was born. It wasn't much, but it was old family money she didn't want my father to take. I couldn't touch it until I was twenty-one. My plan was to get what was mine and hit the road again, but the second I saw you and Jill, my plans changed. I knew I was never leaving."

AJ stood from his chair. He walked over to the end of his bed and leaned against the footboard in front of where I was against the wall. He looked me directly in the eye. "You telling me the truth, bro?"

"Every word, AJ. I'd never bullshit you."

He pursed his lips, and his eyes narrowed. The silence was killing me. "You're a good man, Tate. It took guts for you to come here and admit this shit to me. I'm impressed." He put his hand out, and I shook it.

Relief washed over me. Telling the story I vowed never to utter was painful, but I had to do it to get back on AJ's good side.

"So we're cool then?"

"Yeah man, we're cool. Past is past, but you still have your work cut out for you."

"What do you mean?"

"Convincing me is only half the battle. Now, you have to convince her."

CHAPTER TWENTY-FOUR

Jillian

JAMESON TEXTED ME saying he wasn't going to be able to make it back to work. Considering that horror show slash in his hand, I wasn't surprised. When the afternoon finished, I closed the shop alone. I was exhausted. It had been a bitch of a day and all I wanted to do was go home, take a hot shower, and go to bed. I felt guilty about not visiting AJ, but I knew he wasn't going to start crying into his Cream of Wheat because I didn't show up for once.

A neon pink sticky note stood out against the pitch black of my front door as I approached.

One hundred reasons for me to stay

1. I'm madly, completely, eternally in love with you.

I pulled it off the door and looked down at it. The handwriting was tiny and precise, like the handwriting on so many notes before it. A late summer breeze blew in the air whispering his name into my ear. *Jameson.*

It said one hundred reasons, but there was only one written on the note. It was confusing and weird. Why would he leave this here? More importantly, *when* did he leave this here? His car never returned to the lot after it left that morning.

I opened the door and my heart stopped. Three-inch squares of paper in various neon colors lined the walls. They filled the entranceway of my house, snaked around the staircase, and went up the stairs. I stood in the foyer, my mouth dropped open as my gaze darted around the room. With a shaky hand, I reached for the one marked number two.

2. The only place I feel at peace is in your arms

I tucked the bright green square behind the first one and reached for another.

3. My heart never felt whole until you made your home inside it

Again and again, I pulled notes off the wall and stuck them behind the first. Tears streamed down my face as I read the beautiful words scrawled across the brilliant squares of paper.

12. Your delicious cooking has ruined my palette for all other food

24. You're the best friend I've ever had

I followed the notes up the stairs, my heart fluttering in my chest. The outpouring of love and the time it must have taken him to do this overwhelmed me.

47. You rock harder than any girl I've ever met

55. Your miniature body fits mine completely when we're spooning

I neared the top of the stairs and flickering lights illuminated the dark hallway. Tears blurred my vision, but I blinked through them and continued pulling the sticky notes from the wall.

68. (and 69!) You're a lady on the streets, and a goddess in the sheets

I stepped into the hall; a row of candles shined bright against the dim backdrop and disappeared into my bedroom.

86. My day doesn't start until I see your beautiful face

99. You're my past, present, and future.

I pulled number ninety-nine down just before reaching my bedroom door. For the hundredth time, I wiped my face, and then took a deep breath before walking in.

Candles covered every surface of the room. Their shining lights cast dancing shadows up the walls. In the center of the room kneeled the man who, through thick and thin, never stopped loving me. The more I pushed, the harder he held on. He never gave up even when I did.

The twinkling of a hundred lights highlighted his beautiful face as he gazed upon me entering the room. I clutched the stack of love notes in my hand and fell to the floor in front of him plucking the very last yellow sticky from his chest.

100. There is no life without you in it.

"Cutie, I . . ."

My mouth rushed upon his cutting off whatever he was planning to say. His hands sprang to my back and in my hair as I finally accepted the truth.

We belonged together.

Admitting it to myself was like a weight lifting off my chest. I, Jillian Morello, was utterly in love with Jameson Tate. There was no hiding it. I wanted to shout it into the wind for everyone to hear, to put it on a billboard and have it written in the sky. I wanted to kiss him with everything I had and everything I was.

His mouth pulled from mine and his thumbs padded across my cheeks, drying my tears. "I have so much I need to say. But first we need to talk about this." He reached into his pocket and pulled out a crumpled piece of paper. My eyes went wide when I realized it was the receipt from earlier.

"Where did you get this?" I asked in a strained whisper.

He shook his head and took my hands in his. "I understand why you didn't tell me, cutie, but you need to know we're in this together. You and me. I promise I'll be the best dad and, hopefully someday, husband that you guys deserve. If I have to sell my car and buy one of those mini vans or whatever, I'll do it in a heartbeat."

The blood ran cold through my veins. The look on his face was so hopeful, almost happy. My face fell and the corners of my mouth turned down. "Jameson. The test was negative."

Sadness filled his eyes. "I'm sorry, I just assumed . . ." He trailed off staring at the floor, his smile fading.

"We're going to have babies someday, Jameson. Just not today." His eyes sparkled in the candlelight as they lifted to meet mine. I took his face in my hands and pressed my lips against his in a tender kiss, a promise for a future that I know we'll have together.

Jameson

JILL AND I stayed in bed long after the candles burned out making up for so much lost time. We laid side by side under the covers, our skin fused together so tightly it was hard to tell where her body ended and mine began. A tangled mass of hard and soft that melded together into one singular knot. Our lips brushed together as soft as butterfly wings as I breathed her into my lungs making her part of me forever.

"I love you, Jameson." Her whisper in the dark reverberated against my mouth and wrapped itself around my heart. My fingers ran through her chocolate hair, and she sighed.

"Say it again."

A gray slice of moonlight peeked through the blinds just enough to see the outline of her face and the fire in her eyes. They smoldered like embers as they adjusted to the dark. Her hand ran over my cheek and down my neck to the center of my chest. "I love you. I love you. I love you."

My nose nuzzled against her face and my hands found their way down the roller coaster track of her curvy body. "Can we stay like this forever?"

Her melodic giggle fluttered into my ear. "You promised me a conversation."

"Mmmmmmm," I whined, but I knew she was right. As much as I wanted to lie there entwined with her, I needed to tell her everything. I owed it to her to come clean about my past. Keeping secrets had caused so much damage, and I didn't want there to be anything hidden between us anymore.

I forced myself out of her bed and threw on some shorts, leaning back over to drop a kiss on her head. "I'll make us some food. Come down when you're ready."

Down in the kitchen, I pulled out all the ingredients for the only meal I knew how to make. Tiny footsteps padded down the hall toward the kitchen. "I'm a sucker for a grilled cheese sandwich." She sauntered in wearing my tee shirt and grabbed a water from the fridge.

Joining her at the table, I took a seat across from her setting both plates down. "I saw AJ." Nervousness flickered across her face at the mention of her brother's name. "I know how important he is to you, and I never wanted to be a rip in the ties that bind you guys together. You'd never be truly mine if you were forced to choose, and you'd end up resenting me eventually."

I paused and took a sip from her water bottle before continuing. My sandwich sat untouched in front of me. "He needed to know my feelings for you were real." I reached across the table and covered her hand with mine. "Everything's out in the open, and he's fine with this."

Dampness glittered in her eyes. "You have no idea how much that means to me." Her voice hitched in her throat. "How did you do it?"

"I told him the same story I'm about to tell you." She watched me expectantly as I began to share the sordid web of lies and betrayal for the second time. Her face registered a whirlwind of emotions as she sat quietly and listened. My eyes fell to the table when I was finished. I didn't want her to see the shame inside them.

"Where did you go?" Her small voice broke the heavy silence, and I lifted my face even with hers.

"All over." I shrugged. "South mostly. Made it as far as Louisiana before turning back around. I'd hang out in one spot for a little while, work day laborer jobs for enough cash to hit the road, then move on to the next city. Problem was, of all the places I'd been, none of them felt like home to me."

"Because your home has always been right here." She moved to the seat next to mine and placed her hand over my heart. "You're not meant to be a nomad, Jameson. You're a family man. I've known that since the moment you returned. There isn't a thing you wouldn't do for someone you cared about." Her hand dropped from my chest and her fingers threaded with mine. "Let's make a pact right now. We will both stop living in our pasts and start concentrating on our future."

I looked into Jillian's beautiful face and saw the rest of my life staring back at me. Perhaps fate had a plan for us all along. We needed to taste the bitterness in order to appreciate the sweet. Jillian Morello was more than my sweet. She was my home.

EPILOGUE

I SIT UP in the dark, my shirt drenched in sweat and my hair matted to my head. A grip tightens around my stomach, and I blow out a strong breath. Checking the clock on the table, I watch the time as another fist squeezes around my midsection. My husband lies next to me, sleeping like a log. I exhale a few short breaths as the pain subsides, only to be wracked with another one five minutes later.

"Jameson."

"Are you seriously hungry again?" He stared at me with sleepy eyes and the cutest bed head I've ever seen. I can't help but smile, until another spasm rips through my middle causing me to whimper.

"No, I think it's time to go," I say, trying to remember the breathing exercises I learned in those stupid classes I took.

"Oh shit!" He jumps out of bed and throws on sweats. Even my extreme discomfort doesn't keep me from watching the fluid way his body moves around the room. He is ready for this. Probably more ready than I am.

He runs to the closet and pulls out the bag I have prepared as another contraction attempts to tear me in half. I double over in agony, and he rushes to my side of the bed. "Breathe, cutie. You can do it," he coaches me, blowing out in short breaths. I repeat his actions, and we do the technique together. Strong hands rub small circles in my lower back as he calls the hospital to tell them we're on our way. As I look up at him getting everything together, I can't help but feel lucky. His unwavering devotion amazes me on a daily basis.

Jameson wraps his arm around my back as I waddle down the stairs. Five years ago, he stood in this very house and promised he'd always be with me. He's made me so many promises since then, and he's kept every single one.

A few months after AJ came home from the hospital, Jameson moved into the house permanently. He was always here anyway, so it just made sense. The three of us lived together for the next year. It was one of the happiest times of my life. The two men I loved most under the same roof. One big happy family. When Jameson proposed, AJ felt it was time to go. We told him he was welcome to stay, but he didn't think it was right for us to start our new life together with him hanging around. Jameson and I bought him out, and he was able to buy a little house on the other side of town.

Jameson walks me to my side of the car and sits me inside as if I'm made of blown glass. "All in?" I smile at him as he closes my door and jogs to his side. He reaches over me and attaches the seat belt around my enormous stomach. "Gotta protect my precious cargo," he says kissing my hand as we pull out of the driveway.

When we first found out I was pregnant, he wanted to sell the Mustang, but I refused. That car was what brought us together, and I wanted to keep it. Besides, Jameson loves his car almost as much as he loves me. In the end, we compromised and sold the truck instead. We bought a cheap little SUV. It's nothing fancy, but it runs good and there's plenty of room for all our crap.

"Remember, find a focal point." He glances over at me and puts his hand in mine. I nod and squeeze his hand tightly while trying to breathe through the pain. I focus on the sign in the rearview mirror—Morello and Tate Restoration. The contraction subsides, and I loosen my grip.

After the wedding, AJ drew up paperwork to officially change the name of the business. I was hesitant at first, we'd been Morello and Son's for over two decades, but he insisted the shop was just as much mine as it was his, and my name belonged on the sign as well. In addition to that, if Jameson hadn't stepped in to keep the place going after AJ almost killed himself, we wouldn't even have a business anymore. He worked hard for it and he deserved it. We both did.

At the hospital, they hook me up to the heart rate monitor and IV as I wait for the anesthesiologist to come in with my epidural. Jameson's hand rests on my swollen belly as it clenches again and my hand crushes down on his bicep. "Damn, baby, watch the guns!" he jokes as the throbbing hurt recedes.

"Okay, next time I'll just grab you by the balls." He laughs and pops some music on his phone. He's been compiling a set list of kickass metal tunes to keep me pumped for this. 'Music to push by' he's been calling it. God, my husband is such a dork. It helps, though, and I'm able to focus on the wailing guitar riffs instead of the cramps. When the epidural finally kicks in, I relax back in the bed and spend the last hours together with him just the two of us.

After the shop had been given a much-needed upgrade, we started making changes in the house to make it our own. I lived there for far too long surrounded by the ghosts of my loved ones, and it was time to move on. With the baby coming, we both decided it was time to move into the master bedroom.

Living in my parents' room was weird. I'd been taking business classes at the local university, and Jameson thought he'd surprise me by giving the room a fresh coat of paint while I was gone. The color was awful, and he ended up painting the entire thing a second time. That man is a friggin' saint, I swear.

The guttural noises that fly out of my mouth as I'm pushing out our son are like nothing I could recreate in a million years if I tried. This childbirth shit is no joke. He bursts out seven pounds of screaming pinkness that fill my heart so full, it damn near bursts from my chest and flies around the room. I cradle our son in my arms and look at his wondrous little face before looking up at Jameson. His eyes are ringed red with glistening tears as he stares lovingly down at us both. "I didn't think it was possible, Jill."

"What do you mean?"

"I didn't think I could possibly love you more than I already did. Then you gave me this." His fingertips stroke the soft tuft of hair on our baby's head and he kisses my temple. "I have you, I have him, and now, I have everything."

PLAYLIST

For those interested in my playlist while writing this novel, check out these songs below!

Judas Priest—"Exciter"

Megadeth—"Symphony of Destruction"

Megadeth—"Sweating Bullets"

Megadeth—"A Tout le Monde"

Megadeth—"Peace Sells (But Who's Buying?)"

Spinal Tap—"Bitch School"

Motley Crue—"Wild Side"

Metallica—"Kill 'em All"

Type O' Negative—"Summer Breeze"

Dio—"Rainbow in the Dark"

Anthrax—"Aftershock"

Iron Maiden—"Run To the Hills"

Rush—"Overture / The Temples of Syrinx"

Van Halen—"Hot for Teacher"

Pantera—"Walk"

ABOUT THE AUTHOR

JANE ANTHONY IS a romance author, fist pumping Jersey-girl, and hard rock enthusiast. She resides in the 'burbs of New Jersey with her husband and children. When she's not writing, she's an avid reader, concert goer, and party planner extraordinaire.

Jane loves hearing from her readers! Connect with her on these social media sites, and don't be too shy to say hello!

https://twitter.com/JAnthonyAuthor
www.facebook.com/JaneAnthonyAuthor
www.instagram.com/janeanthonyauthor/
www.pinterest.com/janeanthonyauth
http://tinyletter.com/janeanthonyauthor

ACKNOWLEDGEMENTS

THIS PROJECT IS one that I hold so near and dear to my heart because so much of it is autobiographical in nature. Every character is based on someone I know and love. Jameson and Jillian went from a simple idea in my head, to exploding onto the page in full head banging glory almost overnight. There were times when they seemed to write themselves, guiding the story with me sitting by simply taking dictation. However, I can't give them all the credit. There are so many people who helped me along the way, and I'm so grateful to each and every one of them for their hand in turning my story from a few scribbled lines in MS Word, to an actual real book fit for human consumption.

First, thank you so much to Nichole at Perfectly Publishable for suffering through yet another one of my disastrous first drafts, and for your awesome tips on how to make it better. Your patience while dealing with my neurotic questioning was so appreciated, and didn't go unnoticed. From my obscene overuse of pronouns, to the embarrassing number of times you had to change "alright" to "all right" you powered through, not only making sure every word was perfect, but teaching me to be a better writer in the process.

Also at Perfectly Publishable, I can't forget Christine! When it came time to format this bad boy, I was lost. Even filling out the damn form confused the crud out of me! You walked me through it and made this whole process easier to swallow.

Jenny at Editing4Indies, you squeezed me in at the very last minute to make sure I made my release date, and it was awesome. You stayed up so late. Thank you so much for being so flexible and working with me, and for doing such an amazing job proofreading the manuscript that was so riddled with errors I should be embarrassed. You totally rock!

To Marisa Shor from Cover Me Darling, believe it or not the cover design was the biggest source of stress for me. I agonized over every tiny detail, and drove myself insane. Seeing my vision come to life was the most exciting part of this entire process. You managed to exceed every absurd expectation I had, taking the design to the next level, and made my book more pretty than I ever could have imagined.

Thank you to fellow indie authors Vivian Lux and M. Never for your recommendations, suggestions, and invaluable advice. When I got the idea to publish a book, I had no idea where to even start. You came through like beacons in the dark, holding my hand and guiding me through the process. I harassed the sh*t out of you constantly, but you were always there to answer every question with a smile. (And provided me with excellent reading material when I took a much-needed break!) I have no idea what I would have done without you, and I'm so grateful to you both.

To Jenny, Candy and Devon who beta read for me: you guys rock my socks off!

Jenny—You were the first person I allowed to read it, and I was sitting on pins and needles the entire week waiting for your response. Your enthusiasm for the story came through in all your emails, and made me that much more excited to take the next steps to getting it published.

Candy—There aren't nearly enough words for the amount of gratitude I have for you, lady. Your insanely in-depth, five page list of notes was awesome (and a little intimidating!). Not all of it was good news, but it was constructive, and exactly what I needed to make this book better. Working with you has been a gift, and I can't wait to do it again.

Devon—Your comment "Jillian is you—a teeny, tiny metal-head. Less ghoulish." had me laughing for days, in addition your ribbing about my poor geography skills. (The Sawmill *is* in Seaside! You're right!) When I wasn't begging you for your notes, working with you was delightful. (I'm going to buy you thirty iPad chargers, that thing always seems to be dead!) Seriously, though, thank you so much for taking the time to read through it, and give me your opinion. I appreciate it so much, you have no idea!

Tons of gratitude to Enticing Journeys for putting together the all the buzz, and helping generate so much interest, and to all of the blog writers who liked the book enough to pass it along to their readers. You guys are really the backbone to all of this. Without you, I doubt anyone would have known about it, let alone read it.

Stephanie H! Love love love! Thank you for listening to my relentless whining, and for your never ending support throughout this process. There were times when I didn't think I could do it, but you were always there to offer a listening ear while I prattled on and on and on and on and. . . . .well you get the idea. From my constant self-doubt, to my insane compulsion over choosing a cover (and writing that damned blurb!), you always listened, and never stopped pushing me forward, feeding my insatiable ego with lovely little quips like "You're an amazing writer!" and "You should be so proud!" (I did it! I'm officially the Prettiest Princess!) I couldn't have gotten through this process without you, your friendship, or your guidance.

Special thanks to my awesome husband—my Mustang driving JT in the flesh—for allowing me to shirk every single adult responsibility while I ate, slept, and breathed my characters. You picked up so much slack (and let me steal your computer!), while I sat in a never ending circle of writing and editing until this manuscript was polished and perfect. You are the love of my life, my best friend, and the most wonderful husband a gal could have. I'm truly a lucky woman to have you in my life, supporting every crazy harebrained idea, and giving me the push I need to see my dreams come to fruition.

I can't forget to give a personal shout out to my brother Marc, who was my inspiration for AJ. I got such a kick out of watching you come to life on the pages of my story. It gave me a chance to hang out with you every day, just like we used to before life got in the way. I loved being able to relive watching you play drums in all those crappy garage bands, and jumping the stands during Ozzfest with our crazy friends. I admit, the hospital scenes hit me harder than I thought they would. I literally had to stop at times, because the memories were too hard to even bear. Next to the births of my children, the day you came home recovered was truly the greatest day of my life. You were the first man in my life, and my constant cheerleader giving me support in all my endeavors.

And last (but most important!), THANK YOU to all of the readers took a chance on an unknown author, and read this book. I hope you enjoyed your time with Jameson and Jillian just as much as I did. I'd be lying if I said I didn't miss them once the story was over. I would have loved to see them go on and on but, sadly, their love story concluded, and I had to move on. I hope you fell in love with them as hard as I did, because they deserve to be loved.

39951403R00120

Made in the USA
Middletown, DE
30 January 2017